MARTY'S TERRIBLE, HORRIBLE, VERY BAD DAY

DAKOTA CASSIDY

COPYRIGHT

Marty's Terrible, Horrible, Very Bad Day (Book 17 Accidentally Paranormal Series)

ISBN: 9781797969015
Imprint: Independently published

ACKNOWLEDGEMENTS

Darling readers,

If you're joining me for book seventeen, holy-motherfluf-fin'-smokes, right? Who knew The Accidentals would hang around this long? Back in 2008, when I had this crazycakes idea about a fashion/makeup-driven, kind of silly, maybe even a little dimwitted woman with a big heart who's acci-dentally bitten by a hunky werewolf, I never in a million years believed they'd still be around eleven years and count-less accidental adventures later.

But here we are, and I can't thank you enough for coming back for more time and again! The girls have been through heartache, triumph, tragedy, but the one consistent thing in their lives will always be their friendship.

No matter how many paranormals they've adopted along the way, they've always had each other and their extended family—people Nina calls *framily*—to count on. To many of you, they've become like family. A place you can visit when you want a dose of slang-filled humor attached to some of Nina's foul language, a fashion tip from Marty, or a sympathetic but stern talking to from the ever-sophisticated Wanda. A gourmet meal whipped up by Arch, a warm fuzzy from Carl, or even just a big bear hug from squishy Darnell. In essence, it's a formula that's been rehashed a hundred different ways seventeen books later, and while I wholeheartedly acknowledge said formula, who says formulas (like mac and cheese) aren't as important as the unexpected?

Either way, these characters have endured, and as long as you keep coming back for more, I'll keep writing them until I run out of ideas or my hands fall off (which, if you follow me on social media, isn't as much of a stretch as you'd think. LOL!).

Though, please note, this won't be one of our typical Accidental adventures, in the sense that a new hero and heroine are introduced with an accidental turning. This book is a quickie dedicated to Marty, and picks up sort of where Mermaid left off in terms of timeline and Wanda's pregnancy. As some of you may know, I had a really rough 2017 medically speaking, and spent a lot of 2018 recuperating and getting back on track. In essence, Wanda's still with child since *The Accidental Mermaid* (poor thing—she's literally having the eternal pregnancy. LOL!), and we're just going to pick up right where we left off.

All that said, I'd also like to acknowledge the author of *Alexander and the Terrible, Horrible, No Good, Very Bad Day*. I've rather riffed a bit on this magnificent title. That said, please note, the author, Judith Viorst, has my utmost respect.

Dakota XXOO

MARTY'S TERRIBLE, HORRIBLE, VERY BAD DAY

CHAPTER 1

"*B*looondiiie," Nina Blackman-Statleon crooned softly in her best friend Marty's ear as she lay beside her on her hospital bed. Lights from the werewolf's heart monitor blinked and beeped, and tubes draped from one end of her prone body to another, making her look fragile and small. "It's time to get up, ass-sniffer. I don't have time for this ish anymore, Miss. Everything's falling apart while you sleep like some sorta bleached-blonde Rip Van Winkle. Naptime's over."

The silence filling the sterile room, with its crisp sheets and bedpans and a window of weak sunlight from a frigid Buffalo day spilling onto the floor below, was a deafening roar.

A silence so palpable, it literally knocked at Roxanne's heart as she witnessed the same scenario she'd watched for over a month play out as though it were a song on repeat.

Nina curled her long legs under her and reached a hand up to brush Marty's stringy hair from her forehead before cupping her chin. "Okay, serious talk. What the shit are you doing in there? You do fucking realize that all this time you've been in a coma, your darker-than-Satan's-soul roots are growing in, right? You do remember you're not really a blonde, don't you? That la-dee-da Francoise with the three-hundred-dollar haircuts and the expensive hybrid car would have a shit-in-his-pants fest if he could see how you've friggin' let yourself go. I know if you could see what you look like, you'd shit your pants, too, Marty. So wake up, for Jesus sake. You damn well can't leave me alone with this batch of morons. I need a fall guy. A punch line to my jokes, and you're my favorite little punch line."

Wanda Schwartz-Jefferson, Marty's other best friend, swallowed, the muscles in the long length of her neck strained as she gulped. Pressing her forehead to her arm before she lifted her head, her eyes watery but determined, she held Marty's hand and sighed in teary, very hormonal frustration.

Roxanne knew Wanda's hormones were wreaking havoc with her emotions because on more than one occasion, out in the hospital halls, she'd yelled those words at Nina with clenched fists and matching clenched teeth.

As she sat in a hard chair beside the bed, Roxanne watched Wanda summon the will and search for the right words to beg her friend to come back to them.

"Marty, it's been almost a month. Enough is enough, honey. I can't discount-mall shop without you. Surely you don't think I can bring this Philistine with me, do you? Nina doesn't know a knockoff Gucci purse from a duffle bag. Please, Marty," she whispered, her voice trembling ever so slightly. "*Please*, wake up. We miss you. I miss you..."

Nina nodded, a thick curtain of dark hair falling over

her shoulders and down along her back, her gorgeously lean face pained. "I hate to say it, Marty, but Wanda's fucking right. I don't give a shit about purses and scarves. That's why you need to be here. To give a shit about all the stuff Wanda gives a shit about and leave me the fuck alone so I don't have to *pretend* I give a shit."

"Maybe we're just approaching this all wrong," Calamity, Nina's cat familiar, said rather out of the blue, repositioning her tiny butt at Marty's feet before settling in. "Maybe we need to stop begging her to wake up all day, every day, and start living our lives again."

"*Start living our lives?*" Nina scoffed, her dark head popping up as her sultry charcoal gaze narrowed in on her familiar. "We're doing what anyone would do if their BFF was in a coma, sitting fucking vigil by her damn comatose bedside. So what the fuck do you mean, *live our lives*, Calamity? What the hell else should we do? Throw a party?"

"Well, while Marty loves a good party, that's not what I mean at all. I don't mean bust out the beer bongs and the chips and dip, Nina. I mean, maybe we go about our days like we would if we weren't all stuffed into this hospital room like a bunch of cattle at the 4-H. Talk about normal things, do normal things. Like, don't you knit or something, Preggo?" the cat asked, referring to Wanda, whose swollen belly looked as though she'd burst if you simply brushed up against her.

Wanda's hand went protectively to her stomach, her elegant face showing signs of exhaustion. "I do. I'm not sure how that's going to bring Marty out of a coma, though. Should I knit her a coma hat? Maybe some coma socks?" she asked, her voice snide and angry, and she didn't bother to hide it.

This long haul of a coma had clearly begun to take its toll on Wanda. Each day—until sometimes long into the night—that she came into the hospital to sit with her friend, she looked wearier. No matter how much she straightened her spine to gird herself against the silence coming from her friend's hospital bed, she couldn't hide it in her eyes.

The eyes were the windows to the soul, and Wanda's soul was broken and torn, lost over her friend's illness. And Nina's wasn't doing much better. Marty's coma was sucking the life out of them.

Sucking the life out of them...

Rocky would giggle at the irony of her internal thoughts, Marty and Nina being dead and all—well, mostly dead—but now wasn't the time to giggle at her own stupid jokes.

Not the time at all, Roxanne Evelyn McNally. So she busied herself with the pretend cleaning she gave the hospital room three or four times a day that no one ever appeared to notice and kept her ears open.

The cat sniffed. "Coma socks. That's some funny shit, Preggers. Maybe once you have this kid, you should take your show on the road. Until then, are you ready to listen to my suggestion or do you just wanna dismiss the lowly familiar?"

Wanda rolled her hand in that elegant way she had, her finely boned fingers long and lean. "At this point, I'll take whatever suggestions are available—even one of *yours*, Calamity."

Calamity lifted her hindquarters and huffed her offense by driving her tiny chin upward. "I'm gonna ignore how

4

rude that was and chalk it up to your grief and raging hormones, Miss Rude."

Nina sat up, swinging her long legs over the side of the bed, tucking her raven hair behind her ears. "Get to the point, Calamity. I'm in no mood for your bullshit today. My vampire sleep is all fucked up with Sleeping Beauty, here, on hiatus."

She swished her tail, ruffling the midnight-black fur along her spine. "Fine, fine. Here's what I'm saying. I'm saying, we do the stuff we do day to day, we just do it *here*. So Marty, if she really can hear us like the doc said, hears all the stuff she'd hear if she were at home. Smells, sounds, whatever. So maybe we get Arch in here to cook something and we answer the OOPS phones while Carl reads to Darnell. Maybe we just get the hell on with it. Besides, I think we all know, Marty'd hate this shit, everyone hovering over her for hours on end. She'd want everyone to go on doing what they do."

Wanda's head popped up and she sat straight, twisting the pearls at her neck, her eyes excited for the first time since Rocky had met her—or maybe a better word for what she was doing was *lurked*. She hadn't met anyone officially. She'd simply been observing from a distance and skulking about.

Nina lifted her chin. "What's going on in that fancy-schmancy head of yours, Wanda? I can see the wheels turning."

Wanda slid to the edge of her seat. "Maybe…maybe we bring her *home* and do all those things!"

Nina's face went dark as she glared at her friend. "Home? Are you fucking insane, Wanda? Do you see all the

5

shit she's hooked up to or did you go blind when Heath knocked you up? How the fuck can we bring her home when she's attached to almost every piece of medical machinery there is? Not to mention, she needs round-the-clock care. I love her. Shit, I love her like she's my own damn flesh and blood, but I'm no nurse. I can't change pee bags and tubes and give her all the crazycakes crap they feed her through that damn IV, and neither can you. You're going to have a baby any damn minute now, for Jesus sake. You need to rest, not give our ass-sniffing friend an enema."

Wanda rolled her eyes and hopped up...or lumbered upward, was probably more accurate. As she rose to her feet, she shook her head in a distracted manner and looked out the window into the glare of the late-day sun.

"No, that's not what I mean, Nina. Just hear me out. Look, we're rich, right? I mean, really rich. And Marty's rich. Really, *really* rich. What good is all that money if we don't put it to good use? Let's hire some nurses. A team of nurses, for that matter. And doctors—a team of them, too! It's not like Marty's house isn't big enough to dedicate an entire wing to a staff of medical professionals and all this machinery, right? Her closet alone could house a small country of people. Am I wrong?"

Nina gnawed on the inside of her cheek as Rocky watched her silently contemplate Wanda's idea. Pinching the bridge of her nose, the vampire popped her lips.

"Okay, I'm pickin' up what you're layin' down now. But do you think the doctors here will even let us move her? That one asshole Dr. Doomsday sure as fuck isn't gonna like it. He doesn't like anything, which, under normal circumstances, I'd admire the hell out of, but he cramps my style. I

MARTY'S TERRIBLE, HORRIBLE, VERY BAD DAY

have to sneak past him and ninja in here every time I come to visit her after hours. You should see me Matrix my way through that damn nurses' station. You'd think, this being a freakin' hospital for the paranormal, they'd cut us vampires some slack, but he's got this shit on lock down like it's Attica for the sick."

Wanda frowned, tucking her sky-blue sweater around her engorged middle. "Is Dr. Doomsday a gargoyle or a skinwalker? They've all begun to blend into one big doctor nightmare—except for Dr. Sexypants. *Him* I'd know if I were blind and deaf. That's the other cardiologist on her team, and God forgive me, if I wasn't a faithful, loving wife and a happily married woman, I can't promise I wouldn't give my ovaries a chance to really shine with that dark-haired demon."

"Settle down there, Hormones," Calamity teased with a swish of her tail. "Your ovaries are plenty shiny without Dr. Sexypants in the mix."

Rocky fought a giggle to avoid being caught eavesdropping as she pretended to reorganize the bottles of lotion and perfumes Marty's friends brought so she'd have them if she woke up. Calamity cracked her up.

And actually, Dr. Sexypants was a Phoenix, and his name was Hudson Khalil. A dark-haired, olive-skinned, sultry-eyed, scarlet-and-gold-wingspan-of-at-least-fifteen-feet phoenix.

Just ask her. Rocky could tell you all you needed to know about him.

He was the talk of the hospital, too—not just among his patients, but among the nurses and other doctors. He was *that* good-looking and, above all, kind.

Nina scratched her head and pushed her long, lean body to the end of the bed. "I think he's a gargoyle. But I *know* he's an asshole. A cranky, uptight, hoity-toity, elitist asshole who's lucky as fuck I haven't choked him out yet."

Wanda flapped a hand at Nina. "That's her other cardiologist. She has three who consult, but he's the Chief of Cardiology and if it weren't for him, she'd be dead. So let's not choke him out just yet. He clearly knows what he's doing because at the very least, she's still alive, and if you'll recall, she hung by a thread for a while there while they tried to stabilize her. I don't care how gloomy and curt he is, he saved her."

"He didn't *save her* save her, Wanda. Dr. Sexypants was the real hero at the karaoke bar. Dr. Doomsday just kept her alive when we got her to the hospital. Let's give credit where credit is fucking due," Nina groused with a scowl.

That was not a lie. Rocky had been at the bar that night. She'd witnessed it all. Hudson Khalil had indeed saved Marty. He'd jump-started her heart with compressions and mouth-to-mouth and kept her alive until Nina had scooped her up and rushed her to the hospital.

Wanda frowned. "Either way, Dr. Doomsday is the one keeping Marty alive now, and the man in charge of her care. Dr. Sexypants is just part of the consulting team of heart specialists."

Nina scrubbed a hand over her lineless face and grimaced. "I still can't believe this shit, Wanda. I don't think I'll ever understand how our pretty-pretty princess had a damn stroke *and* a heart attack when she's a werewolf. I always feel like that's the compensation for shedding like a pack of dogs and outliving everyone, we're safe from medical disasters. So how is this even flippin' possible? And doesn't that mean the same could happen to either one of us?"

Wanda rolled her head on her neck to stretch and winced. "You don't have a beating heart, and you don't have working organs either. Which is weird because you're technically still half-human, too. The paranormal has lots of the unexplained and defies logic. But I suppose—because I definitely still have some organs due to my halfsie nature—it could happen to me, too. Dr. Doomsday—er, *Dr. Valentine*—said Marty's technically half-human. She wasn't born a were, so she's susceptible to heart attacks and all manner of things, just like other humans."

"It's because she didn't take care of herself," the vampire spat. "She was all 'Oh, I'm working day and night to keep this merger between Bobbie-Sue and Pack Cosmetics on track. I don't have time to eat more than a stupid celery stick.' Fuck, it makes me so angry I missed the signs. She was having headaches all the time, and no matter how much Bobbie-Sue crap she plastered all over her face with that trowel, she always looked tired. She lost all that weight because she wasn't eating right, and all I did was razz her about how she was a moron for not taking advantage of the fucking fact that she can still eat chicken wings."

Calamity sat up. "I don't think anyone can stop Marty when she wants to do something, ladies," she reminded with a gentle tone. "She was determined that everyone in both companies survive the merger without so much as a scratch. Do you know how many employees Pack and Bobbie-Sue have combined? It was a crazy task to take on alone."

Nina screwed up her beautiful face. "But I saw it

happening right in front of my fucking eyes. I just didn't push her to stop because after the shit went down with our favorite mermaid Esther, she all but holed up in her office so much, you could hardly ever get in touch with her. She even stopped coming to framily night dinner. Who, out of the lot of you that can still eat, ever misses Arch's damn chicken foo-foo or whatever it is? I should have beat the damn door down and made her slow her roll," she rasped. "Hell, even Keegan couldn't get her to relax, and he was as much a part of this whole merger as she was. He *owns* Pack, for Christ's sake. He told me after everything happened, she'd been sneaking off in the middle of the night to work and when he caught her, she told him she wouldn't sleep until she knew every employee, right down to the damn dude who sweeps the floors, was taken care of. It was a shit-ton of pressure."

"But I was the final straw. I'm the idiot who pressured her into going out with us for some karaoke that night," Wanda confessed, her voice shaking, her wide eyes filling with tears. "I played on her sentimentality by reminding her how we used to karaoke all the time. So that much-needed break I hassled her into hassled her directly into a heart attack. I'd give anything to take that night back. *Anything.*"

The raw emotion in Wanda's tight voice made Rocky pause. She hated this part. Hated it more than she hated almost anything else.

Nina slipped entirely off the bed and grabbed Wanda from behind, pulling her friend to her chest and squeezing her shoulders. "You do know it would have gone down anyway, right? She was gonna have a heart attack and a stroke and who knows what else whether it was at karaoke or at home or at the fucking Gucci counter at Macy's, Wanda. Dr. Doomsday said so. Her heart wasn't pumping properly. Her valves were all fucked up and her blood pressure was too high. It was just a matter of time. I'm just glad we were with her when it happened. I got her to the hospital a fuck of a lot faster than some damn ambulance would have."

"I do know," Wanda whispered, letting her chin hang to her chest. "I just wish I hadn't been such a heartless shrew to her before she had the heart attack. I was just so annoyed that she couldn't enjoy two seconds at girls' night with us without checking her texts or…"

Nina squeezed her friend tighter, the memory of the night everything had happened clearly still as fresh as if it were just yesterday. "If the worst thing anyone ever called Marty was selfish, I'd worry. We call each other names all the time, Wanda. It's what we do."

Wanda shook her head, inhaling a ragged breath. "But it was the *way* I said it, Nina. It was the way I attacked. I was *horrid*. God. I was simply dreadful. Was it really necessary for me to scream at her about how self-absorbed I thought she was being in a bar full of people? I mean, I screamed so loud, I thought the man singing 'Born to be Wild' was going to faint from the blowback." Wanda shook her head, her shoulders slumping. "That's not me. That's not who I am. I guess…I guess I was just missing her and it all came rushing at me and caught me off guard…"

"Your hormones were all amped the fuck up, Wanda. You can't help that shit. You're eighty-million months pregnant."

Wanda shook her head furiously, swiping a thumb under

her eye. "No! That's no excuse, Nina. I'm not unkind. I'm not loud or abusive. That's your job."

Nina's perfectly sculpted face took on a pained look, her lips thinning. "Yep, and don't think for a fucking second I don't regret razzing the shit out of her that night, either. I poked her, made fun of her, was a bitch of epic proportions because I was bent outta shape, too. And even if that's normally who I am—even if it's what everyone expects of me—I'd never say another shitty word to her again if it meant none of this had happened—if I knew it would have stopped this from happening. We're both guilty, Wanda. It's not just on you, but we didn't do it to be mean girls. We did it because we love her and there was just no getting through to her."

Wanda reached a slender hand up and gripped Nina's wrist as though it was the only thing keeping her from falling down, and pressed her cheek to her friend's hand.

"But it was my words just before she went up onstage to sing—my last words to her—that I have to live with. I called her a selfish B word. That was the last thing she heard me, or anyone for that matter, say to her, Nina. *What if…*what if she… And I didn't get the chance to apologize? The chance to tell her I didn't mean it. I swear, I didn't mean it!" she sobbed in a raw whisper.

Nina gave her head a vehement shake, her insanely thick, shiny hair rustling along her spine. "Then I'll go to the afterlife and hunt her ass down and bring her back. No way I'm letting that shit happen. Besides, you damn well know, she has to live so we can torture the shit out of her for having a heart attack in the middle of her all-time favorite song 'Push It.'"

"Right in the middle of a resounding *'push it reeeeal good'*!" Wanda said on a watery laugh.

Nina grinned, turning her friend to look at her, chucking her under the chin. "She's gonna shit a Channel bag and it'll make all this waiting around for her to wake up worth it."

Wanda inhaled long and slow, staring up at her friend.

"It's going to be okay, isn't it? No way we can lose her, Nina. There's just no way that can happen. She has too much still to do, and then there's little Hollis…" Wanda choked up again, jamming a finger between her teeth in an obvious effort to staunch her crying.

"My girl Hollis…" Nina muttered, her face returning to its pained expression. "Carl and Darnell and Arch have been with her almost day and night, just trying to keep her occupied. But she's a smart little cookie, that one. She knows something's up."

Wanda nodded, wisps of her chestnut-brown hair falling around her face in disarray. "Keegan brings her every day, and she gets what's going on, Nina. She knows Marty's sick —really sick. But that child, I swear, she's so compassionate, so much like her mother. She read *Vogue* to Marty the other day, for heaven's sake. I can't bear the thought she could lose…"

Nina visibly gripped Wanda's shoulders tighter and gave her a small shake. "Then don't. Don't think it. Don't project. Don't put it out into the universe. For today, right at this fucking moment, everything's okay. She's alive. She's breathing. I know what Dr. Doomsday said, but it's his job to say shit like that. He has to attach all the warning labels to his bullshit diagnosis to cover his ass, that's all."

Rocky silently nodded in agreement as she remade the empty bed opposite Marty's without either of the women even realizing she'd already remade it twice today alone.

Dr. Doomsday had indeed said Marty's coma left her vulnerable and she had a fifty-fifty shot of waking up, and even if she woke up, she could have suffered brain damage due to the amount of time it had taken to revive her. Add in the fact that she'd had a stroke on top of everything else, and was on life support, and she was as close to death's door as she could get.

Dr. Doomsday wasn't a hopeful guy, for sure. He was older and crusty and he'd probably seen more than his fair share of cases like Marty's, but he could at least try and have a better bedside manner. If sucking at consoling a mob of frightened paranormals were a thing, Dr. Valentine would win the trophy.

He was the best in the business. Keegan and the rest of Marty's friends had made sure she had only top-notch specialists. Still, even after a quadruple bypass—which, due to her werewolf half, had already semi-healed—she remained in a coma, and the outlook, if you went by Dr. Valentine's medical ruling, was bleak.

But Rocky, much like Marty's friends themselves, clung to their hope like a life raft. There wasn't much room for hope in her line of work. To see so many people fret over Marty, to see how many people loved her, made her too-soft heart ache.

And where she came from, having a soft heart was as unacceptable as having hope.

It's not your job to hope, Rocky. You'll do well to remember that.

Wanda took a step back and gazed at her friend with a mixture of sorrow and love in her eyes before tucking the blanket under Marty's feet with gentle hands.

"You think she'll like the nightgowns we brought from home for her? I couldn't stand to see her in those ugly hospital gowns one more second."

Nina's face softened, her heartache palpable. "I'm sure of it."

"You're appeasing me," she replied.

"Yep."

"I thought...maybe if we did her hair and put her own nightwear on her..."

"It would help," Nina finished, crossing her arms over her chest. "I get it, Wanda. I'm sure if Marty knew, if she could see what the fuck all's been going on and how shitty her hair looks while she pulls this Sleeping Beauty act, she'd approve."

Wanda leaned her head on Nina's shoulder. "Are you with me on bringing her home then?"

"All the fucking way," Nina groused, holding her fist up to Wanda. "Now, pound it out."

The beautifully elegant halfsie knocked her digits against the vampire's and let loose a heavy sigh.

"Do you think Keegan will go for it?"

"We'll *make* him go for it."

"Nina, you can't steamroll Keegan. You know that. He's enough of a wreck as it is, and he's trying to hold it all together for Hollis and the family. Don't push him over the edge."

"Swear to fucking Christ, if I have to push, I'll push with gentle hands."

"Then it's settled? We talk to Keegan about it tonight? Promise?" Wanda asked, a spark of bright, desperate hope lighting her eyes.

Nina smiled, maybe for the first time since Rocky had inadvertently met her, flashing her perfectly straight teeth. "Yeah, Wanda. We'll talk to him tonight. Promise."

Rocky grabbed the disinfectant from her cleaning cart and sprayed the rails of the bed opposite Marty's and scrubbed it, turning her back to them to hide her concern.

If they took Marty home, that would be great for Marty —not so great for Rocky. How could she possibly keep tabs on her if she was at her house and not the hospital?

It was easy enough to fake being part of the janitorial crew at the hospital, but there was no position she could fake to get her inside Marty's palatial mansion.

And if she was going to protect Marty from her fate—a fate Rocky refused to believe was anything other than bogus —she needed to be nearby so she could watch her and make sure no one else—like a superior or a nosy official—showed up to do the job she was originally sent here to do.

Which was to reap Marty Andrews-Flaherty's soul.

And she was long overdue.

As in, almost exactly one whole month overdue.

CHAPTER 2

*S*o how the hell could she continue to prevent this reap if they took Marty home? This hospital housekeeping job had been an easy solution to her problem while she tried to figure out her *bigger* problem—which was saving Marty's soul. No matter what anyone said—her superiors, her friends, even her overbearing father—Marty Flaherty wasn't supposed to die.

Rocky simply wouldn't accept that. She was an immortal, for the love of the supernatural. Immortals didn't die. That should be their due for sacrificing their human lives—at least that's what she'd been taught.

When she'd shown up at that karaoke bar that night, knowing nothing about the reap other than the location because she'd been late after getting caught up in a Netflix binge and hadn't downloaded the list of souls she was due to collect, she figured she'd just wing it. It wasn't hard to figure out whose soul she had to nab.

Souls weren't hard to identify. They'd be the only dead

17

person in the room. They died, she collected—easy-peasy, right? She'd done it on the fly thousands of times before.

Except, when she'd walked into the darkly lit bar, smack dab in the middle of Dr. Sexypants Kahlil saving a woman's life in the center of the barroom floor, she'd been caught completely off guard.

Partly because she'd recognized the woman whose life was in jeopardy, and it had shocked her, but mostly due to the fact that she also knew Dr. Sexypants—or Hotty McHotshorts, as she'd secretly called him—for more centuries than she cared to admit.

All of it combined had knocked her for a serious loop. Not that she would have collected Marty's soul at that very moment anyway, whether Hudson Khalil had been there to distract her with his deliciousness or not.

Because she was convinced this was some sort of egregious error on the part of whoever made the list of souls due for collection.

So instead of doing her stinkin' job, Rocky had gone home to her tiny cottage on the lake and her dog, Dwayne Johnson, downloaded that stupid list of souls she'd been assigned—conveniently posted on the reaper forums online (reaping was so much easier now that everything was Internet-based)—and double checked.

In turn, as Rocky had stared at the list while picking her jaw up off the floor, her mind had raced in fearful concern.

It couldn't be true. There had to be some mistake, and whoever was in charge of deciding whose soul was on the chopping block—especially one as valuable to the paranormal community as Marty's—had to either have been shitfaced when they put her name on the list, or they had a death wish.

The hate mail alone wasn't worth the reaping, not to mention she could only imagine Paranormal Twitter would be an inferno of hashtags like #FreeMarty and #Reapthis.

But #Donthatethereaperhatethegame. It wasn't her decision who, or was that *whom*, was reaped. She'd never had such a highly visible soul like Marty before, and when folks got wind the cosmos had chosen one of their idols, an immortal to boot, to bite the bullet, she was in for a lot of misdirected hate.

So, because Rocky was so certain it had to be a mistake, and to get in front of the ugly fallout, she'd called headquarters to triple check the validity of the reap.

Yet, she was assured, the soul up for collection did indeed belong to the immortal Marty Andrews-Flaherty from Buffalo, New York, married to Keegan Flaherty, mother to Hollis and esteemed cofounder of OOPS.

Oh, and no one at Reaper Central gave a rat's bee-hind that she was going to be one of the most hated reapers in the history of reapers. She'd been told, quite succinctly, her job was her job, and she could essentially suck it with her protests.

None of that mattered to Rocky, because this still felt wrong. It felt *really* wrong, and it wasn't only because she was a little star struck by the women of OOPS. This reap was wrong with a capital-bad-feeling-in-her-gut kind of wrong. But she had to prove that first. And how did one go about proving a reap, and the jackhole of the cosmos who'd assigned the reap, were a steaming pile of horse pucky?

Worse, how had Marty's name gotten on the list in the

first place? Was it intentional? No one—that Rocky knew of anyway—had the kind of power it must take to change the list, and she'd been reaping for a very long time. The list was the list. End of. It cosmically appeared then you did your job and that was essentially that.

Sure, mistakes were occasionally made. From time to time there was an instance when name confusion came into play, but it was as rare as hen's teeth, and it *never* happened concerning an immortal. Not where a reaper was involved anyway.

Immortals died, yes, but only by special circumstance. An unfortunate garlic incident, a stake through the chest, even werewolves died if a vital organ was hit, but they didn't get the escort of a reaper. Reapers were for human souls.

But headquarters had confirmed it wasn't a mistake...

Fighting a sigh of frustration, Rocky tucked the last of her cleaning supplies in her cart and slipped past the women to head outside Marty's room in ICU, letting the dim lights and cool air of the hallway wash over her.

She was in a real pickle here, and she had no idea how much longer she could stall her superiors before they'd want to know why she wasn't handing over Marty Flaherty's soul.

But every time she thought about the promises she'd made to her boss after her last little incident—okay, *incident* was a tame word for complete fiasco—her fangirl crush on these women stopped her cold.

These women were essential, maybe even critical to the paranormal world at large. They were a force. *Legend*. And they probably had no idea how revered, how worshipped they were in reaper circles, but they were the Beyoncé, Cardi B, and Taylor Swift of paranormal badassery to budding reapers everywhere.

They were a threesome, and asking her to reap one of their souls was like asking her to break up the Supremes. She'd have no part of that, thank you very much. She was not going to be the lame duck at the annual Christmas reaper white elephant who had to explain why she'd broken up the band.

Nope. No thank you, ma'am. These women were the equivalent of the Charlie's Angels of the paranormal world, and even though everyone knew a reaper had no choice but to collect the souls they'd been assigned, misplaced resentments had a way of lingering.

For example, the reaper who'd collected the beloved Mister Rogers's soul, old Horton Greely, still sat alone at every reaper function as though he had the plague. It wasn't *his* fault he was chosen to collect Mister Rogers's soul, but still, he'd been branded an outcast.

"Rocky? Rocky McNally?"

She froze on the outskirts of Marty's room, her hands gripping the cleaning cart until her knuckles turned white.

Oh, that voice. That whiskey-soaked, melt-your-panties-right-off-your-damn-body, make-you-do-stupid-things voice. She'd never forget that voice. To this day, it still sent shivers up her spine.

Not the kind of shivers one experiences when they're spooked, mind you. The kind of shivers that made your knees weak and your heart thump with wild, longing abandon.

It was the voice of the aforementioned Hudson Khalil,

who wasn't just a doctor but a sexy-smexy, bring-you-to-your-knees phoenix, complete with a fifteen-foot scarlet-and-gold wingspan, and the hottest immortal in the reincarnated crowd she'd ever encountered.

Okay, he was the only hottie who was reincarnated that she'd ever encountered, but still, there were few who compared not only physically, but intellectually.

So how in all of tarnation did he know her name?

Turning around, she faced the man she'd secretly lusted after from the moment she'd met him for the first time hundreds of years ago, including as recently as forty years ago before his last reincarnation at the In Between—the place where souls go on their journey to their final resting place.

His strong presence and lightly scented, musky cologne still overwhelmed her, dwarfing everything going on around them. Even after all these years, he still left her with butterflies in her stomach. Those yards and yards of muscles and clear skin kissed by the sun left her unsurprised all the nurses and hospital staff were always gushing over him.

Gazing up at his flawless olive skin pulled taut over razor-sharp cheekbones, Rocky looked into his ebony eyes rimmed with a thick fringe of lashes, hoping she was doing a decent job of hiding her surprise.

Wiping her suddenly sweaty palms on her scrubs, Rocky smiled as though he weren't stealing the very breath from her lungs. "Yes?"

He stared down at her for a moment longer, scanning her face with a half-smile, before he rocked back on his heels and drove his hands into his crisp white doctor's coat. "I was told you were the person who could help me."

Rocky smoothed a hand over her scrubs again and cocked her head. "Help?" she asked, licking her dry lips in nervousness.

Two seconds in a hallway with this man and she was all manner of undone. It was ridiculous. She'd avoided him here at the hospital and everywhere else for this very reason —because he did things to her insides no man had ever done before, and it was damn hard to hide. Harder still to hide the fact that she knew him, but he didn't remember her.

Which hurt. Hurt like the fire of a thousand suns on her skin. But it wasn't his fault. That's what reincarnation did. It made you forget the people you knew and the places you'd been. With some people, reincarnation left lingering memories, that sense of déjà vu, but apparently that wasn't true for Hudson.

He nodded, his dark, slicked-back hair gleaming with the bounce of his head. "Yep. Help. I was just in Mr. Ferris's room, and he's in need of a bit of cleanup. Housekeeping told me you were up on this floor, doing your rounds." Hudson thumbed over his shoulder in the direction of Mr. Ferris's room. "Things got a little hairy in there, literally," he said with a cheerful laugh. "He's a werewolf stuck in shift, and he's shedding like there's no tomorrow. Can you help?"

Rolling her tongue in her cheek, she nodded her head in return, keeping her response short and sweet. "Of course, Dr. Kahlil. I'll get right on that."

Turning her back on him, she scrunched her eyes shut and prayed her cheeks wouldn't go red-hot as she prepared to sweep up after Mr. Ferris, but a light hand on her shoulder stopped her.

"Quick question, if I may?" he asked, his voice gruff with obvious curiosity as he let his hand drop to his side.

Shit. Shit. Shit. She didn't want to engage with him, not even a little. It hurt too much to keep her emotions in check. It hurt a lot. But what choice did she have? As far as he knew, she was an employee here in the hospital, and he was her superior.

Plastering a smile on her face, Rocky turned back around and twisted a handful of her ponytail between her fingers to ground her and keep from turning tail and running.

"Of course, Dr. Kahlil," she offered in what she prayed was a cordial tone.

He paused for a long, agonizing moment, his gorgeous eyes roaming over her face before he asked, "Have we met? I feel like we've met somewhere... Maybe outside the hospital? You seem very familiar to me."

She swallowed hard. Sweet Jesus in a tutu. Had they met? Hah! Boy howdy, had they ever met. But how could she tell him they'd indeed met—over and over—just before he rose from the ashes like a phoenix does during reincarnation, when she wasn't supposed to have met him at all in the first place?

It was against the rules to communicate with anyone when they were making the journey from the In Between to their final destination, even if his destination was earthbound. Her job was clear—escort souls from life to death, period. No dabbling with their journeys, no talking, and absolutely no shenanigans in the interim.

Mingling with anyone other than her own kind was frowned upon. The depiction of reapers in modern-day movies and television was mostly accurate in its solitude.

Swathed in long, dark robes, they gathered souls without a word and aided them to the other side with the point of a finger. But reapers stuck to reapers, period, and if mingling was frowned upon, personal involvement wasn't just frowned upon, it was forbidden.

No one was as surprised as she'd been when she'd encountered Hudson for the first time all those centuries ago. As a phoenix, he was able to freely walk the In Between on his way into and on his way out of his life on Earth. He didn't need a reaper escort due to his inevitable rebirth.

He'd lingered on the plane just a little too long all those years ago, and shortly after she'd dropped off her assigned soul, he'd spoken to her.

And okay, look. He was gorgeous. So sue her, she'd talked back. It started out quite harmless, and she'd double dog dare another reaper to turn her nose up and ignore a guy as good-looking as Hudson Khalil if he did the unthinkable and engaged her in conversation during a soul transfer.

Their conversation had been incredible, and in all these centuries, she'd been unable to forget it—or the ensuing conversations they'd had during his next rebirths, which she conveniently managed to find out about and even more conveniently attend.

But the worst of it all remained: once he left the In Between and was reborn, he forgot all about her and their in-depth, often thought-provoking, sometimes intimate chats.

She'd tested the truth of his "phoenix amnesia" on

several occasions before she'd truly believed he didn't remember what went on at the In Between.

She'd "accidentally" bumped into him at a chariot race in Rome, and in much later years, she'd tested it again by drinking a beer with him and his group of friends at Woodstock.

If he remembered her, he was an amazing actor, because he'd never once let on he recognized her, and she'd honored her reaper code of ethics by not jarring his memory and keeping her distance on the outskirts of any conversation.

There'd been a couple of other times over the years she'd purposely sought him out, but she'd always had the same result. He'd made it clear he had no clue who she was, and she'd left things that way, as heartbreakingly hard as that had been to do.

All that lovesick nonsense aside, why now, after all this time, was he suddenly remembering her? Or maybe she was placing too much importance on what was likely a coincidence. She probably looked like someone he knew. That explanation worked as good as any.

"Rocky? Is it okay if I call you Rocky?" Hudson asked, cutting into her way-too-deep-for-this-time-of-day thoughts. He fingered the chain poking out from his crisp purple dress shirt and tucked it back under the collar.

She vaguely wondered if it was the same chain with the odd-looking charm around it he'd had all those years ago when they'd first met...before she remembered he was staring at her, waiting for an answer.

"Of course, Dr. Khalil. And I don't think we've ever met. I guess I just have one of those faces," she replied, hoping her voice wasn't shaking the way her knees were.

He smiled, affable and delicious, but his eyes were determined chips of granite. "First, please call me Hudson, and I don't think that's it. I don't think anyone could accuse you of being just another face in the crowd."

Now she really did blush; she felt the hot wave sweep over her and touch her cheeks. Instead of screaming the words, "How could you forget everything we shared?" she remained calm and rational.

"Well, *Hudson*, I've been employed at the hospital for about a month. Maybe you've just seen me around. I do clean the ICU, and you spend a lot of time here as a cardiologist, don't you? Stands to reason, me being a background staple and all, I'd become familiar."

He gave her a critical look before his dark eyes lightened and he smiled wider. "Maybe that's it...but I don't think so."

Okay, and? What was she supposed to say to that? Time to nip this in the bud before she couldn't extract herself from a potentially messy situation. It was enough that she'd stalled Marty's reap for as long as she had. Encouraging Hudson Khalil to remember how he knew her was unequivocally off the table.

So she shrugged her shoulders as if this wasn't the man she'd pined over for centuries, and gave him a vague smile. "Well, while you figure it out, I'd better go do my job and handle Mr. Ferris's room. Should I bring in the big guns—wet and dry vac—or will a broom and dustpan suffice?"

He chuckled that husky, warm chuckle of his, the one she heard over and over in her dreams. "I think a broom and dustpan will do the trick. Thanks for helping a guy out."

"Ahem," a grumbly voice, irritated and brisk, whistled into her ears out of nowhere.

Both Rocky and Hudson looked to the left, toward the nurses' station, where the brick wall of a man fondly known by the OOPS women as Dr. Doomsday frowned at them. His bushy brows furrowed, his beady eyes zooming in on them.

Oh, good. The crankiest of all the doctors in the hospital was displeased.

"Dr. Valentine, lovely day, don't you agree?" Hudson said in pleasant tones, giving the overly large, very intimidating man a pat on the arm as though they were old friends.

He frowned at Hudson, his lips thinning in his broad face. "Clearly it's pleasant enough to be consorting with the *staff*." He drawled the word as though it were dirty. As though *she* were dirty because she worked for housekeeping and she wasn't some fancy doctor.

But instead of retorting, Rocky bit her tongue and blanched, her palms growing sweaty again. She couldn't afford to be fired from this job or she'd have no way to keep track of Marty.

But Hudson didn't blanch or even bat a yummy eye, and he definitely didn't bite his tongue. Nay. He smiled brighter, the harsh lights of the hallway accenting the angular lines of his face, making his dark hair darker against the white of his coat.

Crossing his arms over his broad chest, he bumped shoulders with Dr. Valentine. "Aw, c'mon, Dr. V. You know what they say about morale. It begins from the ground up. Rocky's a valued member of our staff. If not for her, we'd be in a real mess. Literally and figuratively. I'm just giving credit where credit is due, along with some friendly conversation. It makes the day go faster."

Dr. Valentine sucked in his cheeks, raised one graying, bushy eyebrow, and gave them both a look of haughty disdain. "And all the while, patients need attending, rooms need cleaning. I suggest you attend to your duties and skip the frivolity. Oh, and do have a pleasant day," he said curtly before pivoting on the heel of his shiny shoe, hands clasped behind his back as he sauntered down the hallway as though he were the king and the ICU unit his kingdom.

Still, Hudson remained unfazed as he looked down at her and comically rolled his eyes. "He's such a drag, huh? Imagine working for all that happy-go-lucky."

Rocky couldn't help but giggle-snort. Dr. Valentine had certainly earned the name Dr. Doomsday. But he also got the job done, and he was one of the top surgeons in the field of paranormal cardiology. She guessed that had earned him the right to be as stodgy as he liked.

"He's definitely not winning any awards for his sparkling personality, but you have to admit, he's brilliant. Not to mention, he's well respected in his field."

Nodding, Hudson agreed with amicable tones. "You can get the job done and still be kind, but word on the street is, Dr. Valentine's not feeling up to par these days. Some sort of gargoyle disease I'm unfamiliar with. Not that it's made him appreciate life more. If anything, it's made him grumpier. So I try and give him a break when a break's needed."

God. Did he have to be so stupid-dreamy? "Fair point. I'll try and do the same."

Now, he backed away, still grinning. "Anyway, thanks for taking care of Mr. Ferris's room. If Dr. Valentine doesn't appreciate it, I definitely do."

Rocky nodded curtly and turned back to her cart, the

sounds of the ICU unit swirling around her, bringing her back to the real world. "You bet, Dr. Khalil."

"*Hudson*," he called after her in cheerful reminder as he swept down the long tiled hall, his footsteps light.

Yeah, yeah. *Hudson.* As if she could ever forget his name.

As if she hadn't tried with every fiber of her being.

As she exited the ICU unit to get a broom for Mr. Ferris's room, leaving the sounds of beeping machinery and the faint smell of Hudson Khalil's cologne behind, she inhaled deeply, her hands shaking.

This was the first time she'd run into him completely by accident, with no nefarious machinations involved, and she'd managed to get out almost unscathed. "Almost" as in her heart would probably beat irregularly for the next week, but she'd survived the encounter.

Now she just had to keep doing that while she figured out how to keep an eye on Marty's soul and keep herself out of hot water for the doing.

And the second this was all wrapped up, she was going on vacation.

An extended, sunny, sand-filled, fruity-umbrella-drink vacation with a bunch of humans who didn't live to be five hundred and look like Hudson Khalil.

CHAPTER 3

"*Y*ou want me to what?*" Hudson asked the very pregnant, soft-spoken friend of his patient, Marty Flaherty.

As he sat staring at the two women and their husbands from behind his desk, he was torn between their request and a daydream about the gorgeous creature he couldn't help but feel as though he knew.

He'd thought about her all day long, fighting to pull a possible lost snapshot from his memory.

Her shapely curves and long limbs refused to get out of his head. All that chestnut-brown hair pulled into a messy ponytail that trailed over her shoulder in gleaming red-brown strands and freshly scrubbed peachy skin he wanted to reach out and caress, felt familiar—comfortable, even.

It felt as though, if he reached out and ran a finger over her rounded cheek, she'd welcome his touch, but that made absolutely no sense. Never mind the fact that it was surely a good way to get himself slapped if he tried to test the theory about her claim that they didn't know each other.

If he'd met her in the years since his last incarnation, he'd certainly remember a woman who had that kind of affect on him, wouldn't he? Wouldn't he remember someone who made him want to wrap his arms around her and kiss her until she couldn't see straight?

Readjusting the chain around his neck, the one he always had when he reincarnated buck naked, he fought to focus on the women and their husbands, but Rocky's face taunted him from his mind's eye.

She was so damn familiar.

And speaking of familiar. The name *Rocky McNally*... That sounded familiar, too. So *why* did her name sound familiar? Why did she *feel* so familiar? Why did she smell so good and why was her raspberries-and-pear scent one he was certain he'd encountered before?

And Rocky wasn't the only person he'd seen lately who looked familiar, who's identity felt like it was on the tip of his tongue, yet he couldn't place them. In the bar where he'd first met these women, he'd casually bumped into a much older guy that he'd swear he knew as he'd elbowed his way to grab a drink.

Maybe his lives were beginning to overlap, and he was just running into souls who had also reincarnated, who he'd known in a previous life?

How the hell could he know if he couldn't *remember* his previous lives?

"Um, hello, Birdman?" Nina crowed, slapping her palm against the top of his desk. "You with us here?"

"Nina!" her friend Wanda chastised with a hand to Nina's arm. "If we were hoping to entice the good *Dr. Khalil* into helping us, yelling surely isn't the way." Then she leaned in, her teeth clenched. "Now, knock it the heck off and play nice. Oh, and quit swearing, you troglodyte."

Hudson fought an inappropriate chuckle. Nina was a full-on beast, an amusing one, but a beast nonetheless. He'd already heard the nicknames they'd given him—like Birdman, because he was a phoenix, and Dr. Sexypants—both of which privately cracked him up.

Even though they'd met under difficult circumstances, and they were pushy and demanding, he'd never regret meeting them.

Karaoke wasn't usually his thing, but he hadn't been responsible for choosing the bar. His colleague, Dr. Harris from Neurology, suggested it, and he'd been more than happy to grab a night out, away from the hospital. It didn't matter where they landed as long as there was a whiskey neat and some cheese sticks involved.

He'd like to kiss the guy who'd invented cheese sticks.

His first introduction to these women hadn't been when Marty had her heart attack, it had been when Wanda, swollen with child, had taken the mic and sung a pretty hysterical rendition of "Rappers Delight" along with Nina, and while there was no way he'd do it himself, he'd laughed and clapped the entire time they'd been onstage.

But it was the moment Marty had fallen to the floor during "Push It" when Nina's true nature was revealed.

When he'd been in the height of compressions on Marty, she'd hovered over him like fried on chicken. Nothing was going to happen to her friend if she had anything to say about the matter, and when she'd scooped up Marty and bolted off to the hospital, he'd been more than a little impressed.

Color him surprised when he'd found out they were the infamous women of OOPS he'd heard so much about over the years.

These women were really something else, and each day he bore witness to the wave in which they descended upon the hospital, his admiration grew. He not only admired but maybe even envied their fierce dedication to Marty.

They never wavered. No matter how tired they were. No matter how frustrated, Marty had never spent a single moment alone since she'd been in his team's care.

Dr. Valentine, crankier than ever before over some disease that left him the last of his kind, had all but shuffled this case off on him, privately labeling it hopeless and "only a matter of time" to his colleagues.

Hudson decided to take on the role of consultant, not because Marty's case presented nothing exciting, or new and innovative to learn...but because he wasn't so sure she was the lost cause Dr. Valentine had labeled her.

First, her brain activity was on point. So was her BP and all the other stats that go along with a healthy paranormal.

It was just something...

Something. *Something* he felt in his gut kept him from giving up hope. Rationally, he realized some of it had to do with her friends' dedication to her. Being the only phoenix in existence to date, he didn't have any family, and though he did have friends here at the hospital, they weren't like Marty's friends.

These friends were ride or die, and he secretly cheered them and their tenacity—he admired the whole slew of them, in fact.

"Dr. Khalil?" Heath, Wanda's husband, prompted from

behind her, his large hands on her shoulders, his face full of questions.

Hudson cleared his throat and sat back in his office chair, the creak of it almost deafening as their expectant silence sat in the air of his office. "I'm sorry. It's been a very chaotic day and I'm still processing. Please, refresh me and tell me exactly what you're offering and what you hope to achieve."

Nina leaned forward and all but growled at him as she eyed him with a narrow gaze. Her T-shirt read "Keep It Up and You'll Be The Strange Smell in My Trunk," and he believed that was a very fair representation of who she was.

Of all the people in and out of Marty's room, she was the most intimidating, and he said that in the manliest manner he could summon while still reluctantly admitting she was a force to be reckoned.

This woman was not afraid to demand the nurses do her bidding or she'd do something ugly to their organs, and she definitely wasn't afraid of grumpy old Dr. Valentine.

If he were honest, even he was a little afraid of Dr. Valentine and the orders he barked like a rabid dog on a chain. But he was a superior doctor, and Hudson had learned a great deal in the time since he'd been here, finally working with other paranormals like himself.

In fact, if it hadn't been for Dr. Valentine, he wouldn't have a job at this particular hospital. He'd mentored him and recommended him for this position. So he was willing to put up with his crabby demeanor and constant demands, for the knowledge he got in return.

Nina eyed him in that scalding critical way that he'd cringe under if he had less pride.

She tapped a lean finger on his desk. "Christ, what is it with you medical geniuses? You're all a bunch of absent-minded dorks. *Pay attention* because I don't have all damn day to futz around with you. The short of it is, we fucking want you to move into Marty's mansion and monitor her around the clock. You'll have everything you need to do it. All those crazy-ass machines she needs to keep her breathing, a suite of your own, a personal chef, Internet, satellite TV, and whatever the hell else you need to make you comfortable. We'll pay you a buttload of money, and compensate you for whatever time you take off from the hospital, too. That means a buttload *more* money. *Capice?*"

Steepling his hands under his chin, his eyes instantly went to Marty's husband, Keegan, who stood in the corner of his glass-and-steel office, overlooking a stone fountain in the square of the complex.

The eerie light of the end of the day, a bruised purple and pink, highlighted the weary lines in his face.

Keegan worried Hudson almost as much as Marty and her current medical state. This large, imposing, dark-haired pseudo linebacker adored his wife. Hudson saw the agony in his eyes every time he sat next to her still form and tenderly held her hand. He saw the pain on his face as he whispered to her late into the night, and when he brought their little girl, Hollis, in for visits.

There was real love between these two people. He felt it every time he entered Marty's room and Keegan was reading to her or brushing his wife's hair, and he wanted nothing more than for them to live out their days together.

It was a love he'd never experienced, and in his many reincarnations, hadn't quite witnessed with the intensity in which he did with them—all of them, for that matter. They all were as devoted to each other as they were to Marty.

Maybe the life-mate thing was real after all, and it made him that much more determined to help Marty get well. But he only had so much power, only so much knowledge at hand to make that a reality.

What he really wanted to know was if this was what *Keegan* wanted for his wife. Hudson got the impression this man wasn't one to be steamrolled—especially as the alpha of his pack. He was accustomed to making hard choices and taking control.

But in times like this, when the woman you loved more than you loved anything else was knocking on death's door, you tended to lose your voice and become overwhelmed by the other voices and opinions surrounding you.

He'd seen it time and again, and he did his best to sort through the emotions so they'd make sound medical decisions based on fact rather than based on what was in their hearts.

Marty's immediate family and their wishes were the most important things to him right now. Sure, he fully understood these women were like family to her, but in the end, Keegan had the final say.

"Keegan? How do you feel about this?" he finally asked, his eyes fixating on his face so he could measure his emotions.

Keegan stood up straight, his full height daunting, but his eyes were riddled with sadness as he crossed his arms over is barrel chest.

His sharp jaw twitched as he scrubbed a tired hand over his eyes. "I'm all for it if you think it will help her. If being at home is something you think will make a difference in her recovery, I don't care what it costs. I don't care what it takes. I'll give you whatever you want or need. I just want my wife to get better. I just want her to come home…"

Hudson watched Keegan swallow hard, and he knew the effort to keep it together was taking its toll on the man. In that vein, he had to be frank with these people and the snarling vampire named Nina, who sat eyeing him like he was the devil himself.

He didn't want to dash their hopes, but he didn't want to encourage them either. The fine line between those two outcomes was precarious at best, and it was the part of his job he hated the most.

Gazing at their tired faces, masks of worry and fear only enhanced by the fluorescent lights in his office, he had to make sure they knew what they were in for.

"You do understand there's no guarantee this will work, don't you? It might not change a single thing. Basically, in light of the generous offer you've made me, you'll just be paying ten times as much as you would for a home health-care nurse."

Nina snorted, curling her lean fingers into a fist, and he wasn't sure if he should duck or prepare to do battle. "You sound like that asshole Dr. Doomsday."

Hudson fought a snicker. Dr. Valentine had been called many things in the time they'd worked together, but Dr. Doomsday was pretty damn funny.

Still, he wasn't wrong about the shape Marty was in. A month was a long time to be in a coma on life support. They hadn't been able to take her off the breathing tube with any success.

But the time could come when a choice about taking her off life support would have to be made, and he wanted them to be ready for that.

Flicking his pen, he looked Nina directly in the eye and forced himself not to flinch. "Dr. Doomsday isn't wrong in cautioning you all. I just want to be clear on where we stand. I'm no miracle worker, Nina. I can monitor Marty. I can order all sorts of meds and handle whatever crisis comes along, but I can't make her wake up. She either will or she won't come out of this."

Wanda's inhale was soft but sharp, her pretty eyes watery, but he had to hand it to her, she was tough as nails for a woman who looked like she was about to give birth any second. She'd weathered this like a champ, and she never veered off the path.

"But you do agree being in her own environment, around her own things and the people she loves could help her, don't you?"

He *did* believe that. He truly believed being surrounded by people who loved you, who'd talk to you and sit with you, was a lifeline to pulling someone back from a comatose state. He'd seen it happen before and it still made his chest tighten.

So Hudson nodded. "I believe that talking to the patient, sharing normal routines, taking them out of the sterile environment of the hospital and into their own home are all crucial to healing, yes, but that doesn't come without caveats, Wanda. Any manner of crisis could emerge while she's this vulnerable. Infection is just one of many that comes to mind. If that happens, I can't support her being out of the hospital. I'd need more help than you can hire—

not to mention x-ray machines and MRI scans and so on. Right now, her vitals are sound, but that may not always be the case."

"But that does mean you'll support it unless something major comes up?" Keegan asked, the hope in his blue eyes searing Hudson's gut.

To most of his colleagues, this would sound crazy, leaving a perfectly good fellowship in cardiothoracic surgery to monitor a rich woman in her home who was on the verge of death.

But he didn't subscribe to the type of medicine his fellow surgeons did. He wasn't always as good at compartmentalizing the sorrow of loved ones as they were and it remained his biggest stumbling block. His compassion sometimes screwed with his reason, and Dr. Valentine wasn't the first mentor to tell him as much.

Yet, the money wasn't really the reason he was considering this offer. Money wasn't why he'd become a doctor hundreds of years ago, and why he became one time and again. He might not remember much from his past lifetimes, people in particular, but he did remember his passion for helping the sick, which always led him back to doctoring in one specialty or another.

He was considering it because he'd come to like these people and their loyalty to Marty. If only all his patients had this many people on their side, the stats for length of hospital stays for the paranormal would surely go way down.

And he liked the work they did in the paranormal community. They were a team, and he was nothing if not a team player.

Looking at them, he rose and smiled. "I guess that's what I'm saying, Keegan. But I need you all to be clear, there may come a time when decisions have to be made. I don't like it, but I would only do you a disservice if I didn't warn you."

From out of nowhere, the surly, oftentimes angry Nina launched herself at him, throwing her arms around his neck and squeezing him so tight, he almost couldn't breathe. Once more reinforcing the idea she could probably take him.

"*Thank you, Doc.* Thanks for helping us bring our girl home," she muttered before just as quickly setting him from her and shrugging off her emotional outburst, straightening her spine and clearing her throat.

"So just make us a list of anything and everything you need, Dr. Khalil, medical and personal," Nina's husband Greg instructed, his hard face a little brighter. "We'll make sure you have it all in place. Name it and it's yours."

Nina dropped her head to Greg's chest and closed her eyes, burying her face in his black sweater as he wrapped an arm around her slender waist and dropped a kiss on the top of her shiny, dark head, pushing the ribbons of thick hair from her face. "It's going to be okay, honey. We'll make it okay. Promise."

Wanda reached out a hand to him and latched on, her warm palm smooth. "Thank you, Dr. Khalil," she whispered hoarsely, squeezing his hand. "I can't tell you how much this means to us. Whatever you want, we'll make sure you have it, and I'll personally see to it you're as comfortable as you would be in your own home."

"And if she can't, I will," Heath offered gruffly.

Hudson's chest tightened at their gratitude—he only hoped he could pull off this out-of-the-ordinary request.

Because he wanted Marty Flaherty to live and prosper and watch her daughter grow.

Probably because he had no roots to call his own, and leaving a child without a mother was the last thing he wanted for Hollis.

He knew what it was to live with no ties to anyone in particular, to leave behind attachments and material items of comfort, and it was a lonely road.

Very lonely indeed.

~

"*T*his is flat-out crazycakes, Rocky. If you get caught—"

"I know, I know, Pepper. You know nothing. You were never here," Rocky responded as she stuffed a pair of jeans into a duffle bag and looked around her small bedroom for anything else she might need. "But I can't just let this go, can I? I mean, this is *Marty Flaherty* of OOPS, for reaper's sake."

Pepper nodded, her shiny hair sweeping over her shoulders. "Yeah. Can you believe how lucky you are to escort someone so famous? Once it's done, everybody will be talking about it for days!"

Rocky made a face at her friend as she reached for her lipgloss on the top of her dresser and sighed at her reflection in the mirror above. "*Lucky?* That's not what I'm calling this reap, Pepper. What I *am* calling it is wrong. Something's not right about this, and I intend to find out what. Sure, maybe the universe wanted her to have a stroke and a heart attack and for all I know, a colonoscopy and a brain scan, but it did not—*does not*—want her to be dead. She's part of the glue that keeps the paranormal world together. She *helps* people. We need her. The paranormal and human world both need her."

Pepper threw up her hands and plopped down on Rocky's bed, pulling at a lace throw pillow and tucking it to her belly. She scrunched up her pretty face as she watched Rocky pack a bag to do what Pepper considered not only presumptuous, but unthinkable.

"There are plenty of souls who help people, Rocky, but they still have to die. That's Reaper 101."

Rocky rolled her eyes and grabbed her favorite after-bath spray, throwing it in the oversized duffle. "But you're talking human souls. I'm talking *immortal* ones here. Immortal being the key word. How many immortals have you escorted through the In Between?"

Pepper stared at her unblinking, her round hazel eyes wide, but she remained silent.

Rocky jabbed a finger in the air to make her point. "Exactly. None. That's how many. And I know the rules, Pepper. I know them well. I'm not some novice."

Pepper waggled a warning finger at her. "Well, if you know the rules so well, then you know we aren't supposed to become emotionally attached to our assigned souls—and that's where your trouble begins every single time. Because you *do* get attached. Remember the really sweet teacher from Pasadena doing that stint for Teachers Without Borders in that remote village in Uganda?"

Rocky straightened and turned her back to Pepper,

taking a deep breath. Yes, the sweet teacher from Pasadena's reap had almost gone awry. Horribly awry.

But in her defense, she had a defense. "He taught sign language to impoverished deaf children in Africa, Pepper. I mean, *deaf children* who'd had no other way to communicate until he came along and taught them. Was I supposed to be supportive of the fact that he was trampled by a herd of elephants? Those kids needed him," she reasoned.

God, she really hated her job sometimes—most times, in fact. Reaping was no way to live out your immortality. She used to lie in bed at night and wonder what it would be like to be almost any other species but a reaper.

"But it's not up to you to decide who lives and who doesn't, Rocky. You're just supposed to collect their souls and call it a day. Your heart is way too big and you're way too soft."

Soft. Sure. She was soft. If caring about the people trying to make the world a better place was soft, just call her squishy. Everyone called her that—the reaper with the heart of gold. She'd been teased constantly for her wishy-washy reaps, but up until now, she'd always stuck to the rules —mostly.

"Well, I'm glad you have no heart and you can collect souls with no regrets, but I saw him with those kids, and he didn't deserve to be trampled by a herd of elephants. So I said so."

Pepper gave her the look—the one that said she was a moron for doubting the universe. "Yeah, you sure did, and because you took so long to collect the poor man's soul while you dilly-dallied with the higher ups, he was stranded in a third world country with some witch doctor who, because he had no medical training at all, thought the best way to heal that selfless, kind, sweet man, was to dance around his jacked-up body and shake his spear at him while he muttered incantations instead of letting him pass in peace."

Rocky winced. Okay, there was that. "He was unconscious when I decided to question authority. He wasn't in any pain. I made sure of that."

That was true. She'd made certain he wasn't aware of anything before she'd gotten on her high horse and bucked the system—for all the good it had done her.

Pepper lobbed the pillow at her. "Is that really the point, my friend? Or is the point that you shouldn't be questioning anything? You should be shutting your face and doing your job so no one gets hurt. And mark my words, if you keep questioning a reap, someone's going to get hurt. Probably *you*—and if you don't, there's still your father who's going to scalp you alive."

Her father. He was a whole other subject for a nice sit-down session at therapy. They'd been at odds most of her life. Because of her compassion for a soul and his lack thereof. He was all business and she was all heart, and the twain never met.

"And that's not the only time something like this has happened," Pepper continued, curling her legs under her and giving Rocky the infamous stern Catholic nun face. "You do remember the hot guy from the In Between, don't you? What was it you called him again?"

"Hot In Between Guy," Rocky responded woodenly.

And did she remember the hot In Between guy? Hah! Sure she remembered. He was all but two feet from her just yesterday, but what she'd *really* remember from now on was the regret she felt for ever telling Pepper about her time with Hudson when they'd met at the In Between.

Pepper nodded her head with enthusiasm. "That's it! That's him. Remember how that turned out? With you crying yourself to sleep for what, two decades?"

Two and a half, but who's counting?

Avoiding the subject of Hudson entirely, Rocky redirected Pepper. "Listen, forget that and focus on the problem at hand—which is an immortal being served her papers. Do you think I really want to be the one to tell that psycho Nina what's truly going on here? Do you think I want to risk her choking me out, maybe even scarring me for life when she yanks my intestines out by way of my nose? But it's the right thing to do, Pepper. Besides, they deal with unusual cases like this all the time at OOPS. It's what they do."

Pepper whistled softly. "She's really as vicious as all the rumors say, huh? I heard she likes animals and children. How bad can someone like that be?"

Rocky lifted an eyebrow and planted her hands on her hips, fighting a grin of admiration. "She's a monster. A monster with a heart, but a monster for sure. I'll never forget the way she snatched up that one night nurse who dared tell her if she didn't sign in on the visitor sheet, she was going to revoke Nina's visiting privileges. Sweet reaper's delight, she had her in a chokehold faster than you can say throat punch. It was insane."

Pepper bit her lower lip, snuggling closer to Dwayne Johnson, who sat next to her in all his canine glory, snoring. "She's going to kill you."

"She can't kill me. I'm immortal."

"She can if she whacks your head off. It's our one weakness, but even if she doesn't, she's at the very least going to rip you limb from limb, and then you'll be a limbless immortal."

"Then I'll be a limbless immortal who still has most of her faculties. I don't need much. But at least I'll have made the effort. I can't just let this go without investigation, Pepper. And might I remind you, it's not your head on the chopping block here, sister. It's not you who'll have the entire paranormal world hot on your heels for taking an immortal's soul—a *revered* immortal's soul. It's mine."

Pepper sighed, twisting a strand of her mahogany hair around her index finger. "I know, I know. I totally get it. Your heart's bigger than your brain. And I still don't understand how an immortal got on the list to begin with. It makes no sense."

Damn right, it didn't make sense. "The only explanation I can come up with is the fact that Marty's only half paranormal. The human half of her, the one susceptible to human ailments, is the part of her soul that triggered the reap."

Reaching upward, Pepper stretched and grabbed a T-shirt from the pile on Rocky's bed, folding it neatly before she said, "Now that does make sense...and by the way, I *don't* envy your position. Not one bit."

Looking around her bedroom, in all its soothing blues and creams, a color common for reapers due to the stress of their jobs, Rocky nodded and smiled at her friend. "So I can count on you to cover for me?"

"You can always count on me, Rocky. *Always*. But I was

still never here," she said on a nervous chuckle, her hazel eyes scanning the room as though she expected someone to pop out of her closet. "Consider me your distant support system. And I still say, asking those women if you can move into Marty's McMansion and babysit her soul, while you try and figure out how she got on the reaper list to begin with, will be met not only with skepticism, but maybe even some violence."

Yeah. This was likely going to be a hard sell. But she had her reaper robe and magic scythe as proof of who she was.

That should be enough, shouldn't it?

CHAPTER 4

*A*s she rang the bell to Marty's insanely beautiful home, Rocky decided she either had to find a new line of work or build her own cosmetics company, because wowee—this was some serious crib, and she had some serious crib envy.

At a glance, Marty and Keegan Flaherty's house was magazine perfect in a darkish blue with walnut wood shutters and varied gray accents that didn't reflect how enormous it was until you got up close.

Tall, rounded pillars lined the long, decoratively paved porch in gray and rust—each pillar sporting a potted topiary in a rustic-looking pot beside it. As the frigid winds of winter blew at her reaper robe, Rocky took in the beautiful stained-glass insert of the double doors with a mosaic picture of colorful hummingbirds in flight and admired the smooth teak finish.

Enormous Adirondack chairs with small tables between them created vignettes of cozy warmth, making Rocky wonder how many summers they must have spent here, looking out over their football-field-sized front lawn.

Wind chimes hung sporadically from the porch's ceiling, and some kind of vine, now dormant in the winter, wove over the rails from the garden below the porch.

Now that she was here, now that she was up close and personal, her heart did a nervous dance in her chest.

Maybe Pepper had been spot on. Maybe this was a huge mistake. Maybe the cosmos was right and Marty was supposed to die, and now Rocky would die with her because Nina was going to slice her head off with her own scythe when she heard her tale.

Maybe.

And maybe it's just nerves, Rocky. Maybe you need to man the hell up, balls to the wall go with your gut. Stick to your guns. Show 'em who's boss.

And if all else fails, there's always Dwayne Johnson. Who could resist his sweet little half bulldog/half pug face?

No one—no demon or contrary half vampire/half witch anywhere in the land—could resist that wrinkled face, that's who.

Kneeling down, as the wind blew and the dark clouds formed, she cupped Dwayne Johnson's face lovingly. "I need you to be extra cute here, pal. Like pour on the cute so mama doesn't end up with no head, okay? Nina loves animals. Make her love you the way I do."

Dwayne Johnson grunted and licked her hand before dropping down at her feet to spread his legs and thoroughly clean his southerly parts, totally unaffected by her plea.

She gave him a pat on his tan and brown back and rose, straightening her shoulders.

Two things can happen here, Rocky. Either you die, or you live with some serious deficits. Drinking through a straw for eternity won't be the worst that can happen to you. Stop being so farkin' selfish and get on with it. It's a disservice to the paranormal community if you don't at least look into this.

One deep breath later, she hauled her backpack closer, tightened her hold on Dwayne Johnson's leash and her trusty scythe, and rang the doorbell. Pulling the hood of her reaper robe around her face, she fought a shiver.

The elderly gentleman named Archibald—or Arch, as everyone in the group called him—answered the door with a question in his eyes, his flawless black suit jacket and shiny shoes sparkling even under the gloomy skies.

She'd wondered since she'd covertly witnessed this group at the hospital if Archibald was paranormal. There were no outward signs then, and there were none now.

"Good afternoon," he said, articulately cordial, his hands clasped in front of him.

Swallowing hard, she replied, "Good afternoon."

And then they stared at one another in uncomfortably awkward silence as the wind blew and the day grew shorter.

This was not going as planned.

But Archibald broke the ice so she didn't have to. "I know I'm ancient, Miss, and my memory isn't nearly as sharp as it once was, but surely Halloween has long past," he said with a half-smile, his tone clearly teasing as his eyes swept over her reaper robe and scythe. "How may I be of service?"

She'd laugh if she wasn't so dang freaked out right now. It was one thing to play this little scenario out in her mind, quite another to actually make it happen.

Licking her dry lips, she smiled at him. "Your memory's just fine, sir. It's not Halloween at all. My name is Rocky McNally, and I'd like to speak with Wanda Jefferson and Nina Statleon, please."

Archibald assessed her in his ultra-proper way with a haughty glance. "They're quite busy at present. Maybe I can be of help to you?"

"No. No, you can't help me at all," she blurted as Dwayne Johnson rudely slurped his way along his back leg, making an ungodly amount of embarrassing noise. "I need to speak directly to them and only them. If you'd just tell them I'm here, and that it has to do with their friend Marty, I'd really appreciate it. It's super important I talk to them. Super, super important. *Vitally important.*"

Dear God, she should have practiced this speech before she showed up, looking like an idiot and sounding worse, dressed in her reaper robe, which, for all intents and purposes, could have been bought at the local Walmart.

Now Archibald's antenna was up and on alert. He squinted his soft blue eyes and lifted his sagging chin. "Please wait here," he said curtly, shutting the door behind him.

She let her forehead rest against the side of the house, her cheeks hot, her mouth like the Mohave. Stupid. Stupid. Stupid. Her intro had been weak at best. No way they'd let her in now.

No way she was—

A firm hand stopped her internal fretting as it grabbed her by the front of her robe and literally hauled her inside, slapping her up against the wall in the entryway. Everything went blurry as the back of her head slammed into the wall, making her teeth clack together.

And then, surprise of all surprises, it wasn't Nina staring back at her as she'd expected. It was *Wanda*, sans her usually serene face, her nostrils flaring and her artfully made-up eyes bulging with flashing fury.

"*Who the hell are you and what the hell do you want?*" she demanded through a tight jaw.

And all Rocky could think of was, holy cow, this was Wanda Schwartz-Jefferson, *the* Wanda Schwartz-Jefferson, knocking her around like a punching bag. Oh, the stories she'd tell. After her concussion healed, of course.

"Wanda! What the fuck?"

Through blurry eyes, Rocky saw Nina come up behind Wanda and put a hand on her shoulder, patting it. "Whoa there, Preggers. Ease up. Threats are my job. You have a bun in the oven to protect. Now chill and let me handle this."

But Wanda's eyes narrowed and she shook her head. "I said, who the hell are you? Answer me or I'll make you wish you were dead!"

Nina's eyes flew open in surprise as she clucked her tongue in admonishment. "Whoa-ho there, little lady. What the fuck's gotten into you? Put the kid down, Wanda. I can't believe I have to tell you this. Are we in some alternate dimension where I'm teaching you fucking manners?"

But Wanda wasn't letting go. Nay, in fact, she gripped tighter and shook her, making Rocky's eyeballs cross. As she hung there, pressed against the wall, her legs dangling, one of her clogs halfway across the floor, Nina reached around Wanda and began to pry her fingers one by one from Rocky's robe.

"Wanda, I said *let go*. Let go now, or I'm going to drag your ass out of here by your perfectly groomed hair. Ease off and put. Her. Down," she hummed in her friend's ear with a snarl.

Wanda let go so suddenly, Rocky had no time to brace herself before she dropped to the floor like a rag doll, knocking over a nearby table and its contents with her flailing legs before the back of her head whacked the wall behind her.

"Rocky?" a deep voice called as she heard footsteps pounding down the stairs to her right.

"You know her, Hudson?" Wanda asked, backing away.

"I do. She works at the hospital," Hudson Khalil said as he knelt down in front of her and pressed gentle fingertips to her head before using a thumb to pull her eyes open. "Rocky? Are you okay? Answer me, please."

She looked up into his sharply angled face, her eyes crossing, but still able to see how incredibly good-looking he was—even through what she'd surely classify as a concussion.

Swatting at his hands, she tried to melt into the wall at her back to avoid his touch. Why was he suddenly everywhere she was? "I...I'm fine," she said on a wince as he offered a hand to help her up.

"The hospital?" Nina balked with a frown and a huff. "Is she here for you? Arch said she wanted to talk to Wanda and me. Who the hell are you?"

As Hudson helped her rise, his big hand still holding hers, she heard him say, "Maybe we could give her the opportunity to tell us rather than knock her clear across the room?" Quite aggressively, if you asked Rocky.

"Oh, shut your sound, Birdman." Nina flicked her long fingers in his face. "We were just doing what we do when someone suspicious shows the fuck up unannounced."

Instantly, Wanda's beautiful face looked horrified. Her hand went to her throat and the necklace she wore as she twisted it in her fingers. "Oh heavens, I'm so sorry! I don't know what's happening to me. Please…" She gestured to the kitchen, which was directly ahead of them. "Come in and sit down and we'll make you some tea. Do you like tea? Or would you prefer something else? Hot chocolate? Coffee? Maybe something cold…?"

As Wanda's voice trailed off toward the kitchen, Rocky remembered poor Dwayne Johnson, outside in the icy air. "My dog," she managed to mutter through the throb of her head.

Hudson pointed to the grand fireplace in the middle of the living room, covered in beautiful white and gray stone. There, Dwayne Johnson sat curled up in a marabou-lined pink dog bed that was much too small for his overfed bulk, reveling in the warmth of the roaring fire.

"I take it that's your dog?" he asked with a charming grin as he looked down at her with eyes of concern.

She inhaled a ragged breath and rolled her head on her neck. "Yes. That's Dwayne Johnson. I'm sorry. I'll get him. He has no shame. A bed's a bed, pink and frilly, it makes no difference."

"Leave him," Nina ordered, sticking out a hand to prevent Rocky from collecting her dog. "He'll be fine, won't you, Dwayne Johnson?" she cooed in the dog's direction, making kissing sounds. "Who's a good-good boy?"

Vaguely, Rocky gave pause when she discovered the

rumors that Nina appeared to love animals and children were true—before she realized she was still holding Hudson's hand.

And it felt good, and warm, and reassuring, and that was not good and not really reassuring at all.

She didn't want to get caught enjoying Hudson's touch or making googly eyes at him. That was and always would be a no-no.

Rocky's heart crashed in her chest in fear as she snatched her hand back. She lifted her chin and looked to the open kitchen area, where Wanda flitted about, and made her way in that direction on wobbly legs as fast as she could.

Wow, Wanda packed a serious punch. She rubbed the knot forming at the back of her head and stood on the threshold of the kitchen. The glorious, enormous, cream-and-antique-black kitchen, with a white farmer's sink and an island the size of her bed, was as beautiful as one would expect.

As she absorbed the beauty of her surroundings, taking in the fresh flowers in the middle of one long length of glossy countertop and the basket of shiny red apples at the other end, she inhaled in the hopes a cleansing breath would ease her anxiety.

"Please, Rocky, is it? Do sit down, Miss, and let me make you comfortable," Archibald insisted, handing her an ice pack and ushering her to the long wooden table, bleached white and antiqued to a rosy glow.

Wanda's shoulders sagged in defeat as she looked at Rocky, clear remorse in her eyes. "Please don't be afraid of me. I just reacted. I'm not sure if you know what we do, but we have enemies, and we didn't know who you were or what you wanted and…"

"I… I know who you are. That's why I'm here," Rocky said, hesitantly slipping into one of the softly upholstered, beige-cushioned chairs in black wood and iron.

Across the table, Nina dragged a chair out and sat down, driving a finger into the top of the wood. "Explain," she demanded with narrowed eyes. "And while you're at it, explain the fucking Halloween costume, too."

"Nina," Hudson interrupted, his cologne filling her nose as he sat down next to Rocky, draping an arm around the back of her chair. "She's just had quite a crack to the head. Can we give her a minute, please?"

Her cheeks flushed warm and hot at Hudson's defense of her, but she wanted to get this over with as much as they wanted to know what she was doing, intruding on their later afternoon.

As Wanda set a mug of hot tea in front of her, Rocky rolled the sleeves of her robe and took a deep breath. "All I ask is that you let me explain everything before you react and throw me against another wall."

Wanda's eyes immediately teared up as she reached over and squeezed her arm. "I'm so sorry, Rocky. I can't explain why I'm behaving so poorly. My only excuse is I've been pregnant for what feels like forever and my hormones are on a hormones-gone-wild escapade that's spun out of my control. I promise we'll hear you out."

"But I can't fucking promise I won't throw you up against another wall when you're done," Nina growled.

Rocky winced, but she managed to fight a cringe. "Fair enough. I'll take my chances." Wrapping her cold hands around the warm mug, she began, "Anyway, my name is Rocky McNally...and I'm a reaper. A grim reaper..."

~

*A*n hour later, as everyone sat around the table stunned and wide-eyed, Rocky folded her hands together to keep them from shaking, waiting for them to get past the initial shock of Marty's fate and begin the interrogation she was sure she was in for.

The good news? She'd survived liftoff. Now she just had to convince them to let her hole up here in order to protect Marty while trying to find out what the hell was going on.

"So lemme get this shit straight. You thought you could prove to us you were a damn grim reaper if you wore your reaper shiz?" Nina asked on a cackle. "Like, seriously?"

"Nina! That's your takeaway from everything she just told us? You *did* hear her say Marty's soul is in imminent danger, didn't you? And she's the one assigned to cart our best friend in the world off to this In Between?" Wanda hissed. "Forget about what she's wearing, Elvira, and focus on the problem. Keeping Marty's soul *in* her body."

Nina lifted her middle finger at Wanda. "I'm just saying, her paranormal game is weak. I have fangs and you shed like a dog. She has a stupid fucking coat you could buy at the Dollar Store."

Hudson held up a broad hand, his gaze going from Nina's to Wanda's faces. "Let's hear her out, ladies, yes? This could explain what's happening with Marty and why she's in this deep state of sleep. Maybe her condition really has

58

nothing to do with a medical issue at all. So give her a chance."

Aha. Rocky hadn't thought of that. Maybe Marty's soul was suspended, or something sci-fi-ish she didn't understand.

Fiddling with the edges of her robe, she muttered, "I don't know whether what Dr. Khalil—"

"Hudson," he cheerfully corrected her again. "It's just Hudson."

"Okay, then I don't know if what *Hudson* says is true, because I've never, in all my time as a reaper, come across anything like this. We don't escort immortals over the threshold. It's just not done. I don't know who does, because I imagine they're few and far between, but my gig is human souls, and that's why Marty's set off some red flags for me."

"And you think the way to keep her soul from harm is to watch over her?" Hudson asked, his warm voice filled with concern.

Bobbing her head, Rocky grimaced. "I do. I know it was presumptuous of me to show up here like I did, with my dog and my bag packed, but I'm—pardon the pun—deadly serious about guarding Marty's soul. I did the best I could at the hospital while I pretended to be part of the house-keeping staff, but when you all decided to move her, I knew I had to act."

"So your plan is to keep other reapers at bay if they decide to take it into their own hands and reap Marty's soul?" Wanda asked, her brow furrowing.

"I know it sounds crazy, but the universe is going to want a soul—and it'll want it soon. I can't let that happen until I know for sure there's been no mistake."

Nina leaned across the table and glared at her, flashing her pointy vampire teeth. "But there *has* been a mistake. *A big fucking mistake.* Nobody's taking anything on my watch, and they're definitely not taking Marty."

Rocky sighed. If only that were the way it worked. If only brute strength and enough rage for ten men was the way to keep a soul from collection.

"What if another reaper shows up to collect her soul?" Hudson asked, his eyes searching hers. "Do you duke it out or something to prevent it?"

Okay, she hadn't thought that far in advance. So she shrugged and shook her head to show her confusion. "If that's what it comes to, I guess I will. I'll do whatever I have to in order to prevent Marty from being collected. I don't care what the cosmos tells me, this reap is wrong. Something's gone wrong. I just don't know how to figure out what exactly the 'wrong' in the equation means."

Nina cocked her head, her gaze locking with Rocky's, her eyes full of menace. "Props to you for having the balls to stick to your convictions—or are they delusions? I mean, how the fuck are we supposed to know if you're telling us the truth or you're just some bananapants nut, stalking us? Because we've had a coupla those in our time, and I'm here to tell you, that didn't work out so well for the stalker. How can you prove you're who the fuck you say you are?"

Her scythe. She didn't have magical powers per se, other than the ability to walk the path of the In Between, and she couldn't take them there—she wouldn't be allowed entry by the gatekeeper simply because she wanted to show them it existed.

She also didn't have outrageous strength like Nina, and

she couldn't shift the way Wanda and Marty could…but she did have her scythe, which was a mighty powerful weapon, and probably the only form of proof she had.

Twisting her body around, Rocky looked toward the area of the front door. She'd lost track of her scythe, a big no-no in the reaping world, not to mention, dangerous. "Do you know where my scythe got to? I can show you, if that's okay?"

"Do you mean this?" Heath asked as he entered the room, holding her scythe in his strong hands, the gleaming gold and silver of the handle virtually glowing in the weak sunlight pouring in from the cache of windows over the kitchen table.

Rocky nodded, rising with slow, measured movements— so no one would attack—to let Heath hand her the scythe.

"Do you all mind coming out into the backyard? I don't want to make a mess in your beautiful kitchen," Rocky asked, not even bothering to wait for an answer as she made her way to the back door, turning to look at them before taking a step outside to the gorgeous patio, where tons of toys and even a plastic castle sat on decorative pavers.

As they all gathered on the patio, facing the line of trees at the edge of the property, she caught sight of Hudson, standing protectively on one side of Wanda as though to shield her, while Heath flanked her other side.

Rocky's heart skipped a beat. She still didn't understand exactly why the heck he was here at Marty and Keegan's, but she didn't hate that he'd defended her or that he was so handsome when he'd done so.

Nina gave her shoulder a hard shove and frowned, her lips a thin line. "Okay, Reaper, and…? What's fucking next?"

Lifting her scythe over her head, Rocky gave them a warning. "You all might want to back away and give me some room. Oh, and cover your ears. For your own protection, of course. Especially you, Nina. Vampire hearing and all."

With that, she turned her back on their skeptical eyes and faced the row of barren trees, spreading her legs and widening her stance to brace herself for impact.

She gripped the handle of the heavy steel weapon tight and, using her wrists, pointed it at one fairly isolated but rather oversized maple tree, winding up with a swing.

The buzzing sound the swing of her scythe made, often compared to thousands upon thousands of angry bees, grew with each arc in the air, making Nina cry out.

"Fuck! Knock it off!" she screeched, clamping her hands over her ears, wincing in obvious pain.

With a flick of her wrist, Rocky let 'er rip, shooting an arrow of blistering-white light at the tree, effectively slicing the maple in half.

The eerie silence just before it fell was almost poetic, as the thick base of the tree and its trembling limbs hovered in the air seconds before crashing to the ground with a heave and a groan.

The crash and the ensuing rubble of debris and dead limbs it left behind made everyone stand stock still, all of them unblinking.

"Well…ain't that some shit?" Nina finally said, her voice hoarse. "Okay, so you have a magic sword—"

"Scythe. I have a magic *scythe*," Rocky corrected, feeling a little less powerless and fragile. She never used it much, not as a weapon anyway. That wasn't what it was used for. The scythe was actually an agricultural representation of reaping crops that had somehow translated to cutting people down, but she'd had it since forever, and in a pinch, it could create quite a ruckus. She never did a reap without it. "And it's all the proof I have that I'm a reaper, and I'm here because I want to protect Marty's soul."

Heath whistled as Hudson openly gaped at the pile of tree debris.

"Well then," Wanda said with a pale face and a quick pat to Rocky's back before brushing her hands down over her skirt in a nervous gesture. "Let's get you settled in a room, yes?"

"Scythe-schmythe," Nina sneered as she brushed past her on her way back inside, knocking Rocky's shoulder as she went. "You do that shit again and I'll break that fucker in half and shove it down your pie hole, *Reaper.*"

Rocky stood for a moment as everyone dispersed and inhaled the frigid air, fighting the shake of her legs and the chatter of her teeth.

Then she smiled in fangirl appreciation at Nina's notorious grumpiness.

Wasn't it awesomely gratifying to find your idols were everything you hoped they'd be and more?

CHAPTER 5

"*S*o what the ever-lovin' fuck now?" Nina asked her as they sat together on the thickly carpeted floor of a small sitting room just outside Marty's room, where Hudson checked her vitals and tweaked her IV line, while Wanda slept and Nina took the night shift.

Yeah. What now, Rocky?

You've made your big entrance, showed them what you've got. Next, please.

The trouble was, she didn't know *what now* any more than anyone else. She was flying by the seat of her pants. Still, honesty was always the best policy.

"I honestly don't know, Nina. I don't know where to turn from here. I checked with all the appropriate people about the validity of Marty's reap, and everyone's told me the same thing. I guess I have to find out who or what determines the list of souls due for collection, and I'm being straight with you when I tell you, I truly *don't* know who or what that is. So we wait."

She had a funny feeling that wasn't what Nina wanted to

hear, because she was all about kill first, ask questions later, but it was all they had. The best she had to offer was preventing the reap.

"Wait," Nina grunted. "I'm shit at waiting for something to happen. If you point me in the right direction, I'll kill the fucker and we won't have to wait anymore."

Rocky nudged the vampire's knee. "I can't point you to someone when I don't know who that someone is, Nina."

"Stop making goddamned sense. It pisses me off."

"What doesn't piss you off?" she asked with a teasing smile.

Nina glared at her, running her tongue over her lips. "Salty reaper is salty."

Rocky grinned. "I'm just keeping it real, and the reality is, I don't know what to expect or what to do."

Nina rubbed Dwayne Johnson's filled-to-the-brim-with-table-scraps-from-the-delicious-dinner-Arch-had-cooked belly, and grimaced. "You don't know who creates this fucking list? How can you not know that? I mean, where the hell does this list come from to begin with?"

Rocky sighed, scooting Muffin, Marty's tiny poodle, over a bit and crossing her legs, her temples showing the early signs of a headache. "It just appears and I download it and it leaves no digital footprint. It's cosmically generated, and I've never once questioned it. I know that sounds crazy, but liken it to brushing your teeth or taking a shower. You just do those things because that's all you've ever known. The list just is."

"Listen, I can't cast stones at glass houses. There are so many fucking things that just *are* in this crazy-ass world, I believe you when you say you don't know why the fuck it exists."

"Though," Rocky said, holding up a finger. "There has to be someone who monitors it, right? I mean, I do have superiors. So, I figure that someone will probably show up sooner or later when I don't deliver Marty's soul…"

She hoped. Sort of. It meant a shitstorm of trouble for her, but she could live with trouble if it meant she was doing the right thing.

"So why don't you give these fucks a ring-a-ling and let me talk to them about what's going on?"

"Because I'm hiding in plain sight. No one's asked where Marty's soul is yet. If I can find out who's responsible for putting her name on the list before I rock the boat, I'm opting for smooth sailing."

Why no one had shown up so far remained a mystery, and she wouldn't question it, but she couldn't expect her luck to hold forever.

"Understood. A good plan." Then Nina's eyes went hard. "So should I prep to rip someone limb from limb? Like, how the fuck are we supposed to keep this shit from happening? I feel like I'm chasing shadows here. How do you keep a soul in someone's GD body, for shit's sake?"

Rocky sighed and stared off at the mirror atop a long, glossy black cosmetic's vanity beyond Nina's shoulder, where there was a ton of Pack and Bobbie-Sue cosmetics, neatly stacked in a bright array of glamorous packaging.

"I can't answer that, Nina. Like I keep saying, I've never had this happen before. I don't know what to expect because I've never not delivered a soul."

But it made her stomach hurt to think about it. Not as

much as it hurt to think Marty was being reaped unfairly, but it hurt nonetheless.

The best she could figure was a higher up would come calling, and she'd be in hella trouble up to her eyeballs. Reapers had a prison just like the rest of the world did, but if she ended up peeing in front of an audience for eternity, at least she wouldn't have been the person to take such a valuable soul.

Nina grunted, her jaw hard and tight. "So lemme get this straight. Basically, you should have fucking collected her soul at the bar, right? She was technically dead then?"

Watching Nina avert her eyes, hearing the words come from her mouth and knowing they hurt, made Rocky wince. But she wanted to keep everything above board.

She let her chin fall to her chest. Guilty. But she wouldn't apologize for hesitating. Her heart told her she'd done the right thing.

"Yes. According to the rules of the reap, I should have collected her soul in that moment."

Nina leaned forward, her long, silky hair partially covering her face, and thumped Rocky's leg. "But you didn't," she said, her voice almost on the verge of shaky. "Color me fucking grateful, kiddo."

Rocky remained silent, uncomfortable with praise from someone she admired so deeply. Instead, she looked down at her sneakers and fiddled with the laces, noting how frayed they'd become.

"*Why* didn't you collect her soul?" Nina prodded. "Why are you sticking your neck out for the lot of us?"

"Because she's an immortal," Rocky mumbled. "And because I know in my gut it's wrong. You three are legends where I come from—you're legends in the paranormal world. You not only help people who've been accidentally turned, but you've prevented more than your fair share of catastrophes. I'm not going to take an immortal soul and live with the guilt of that until I know it's the right thing to do, especially when all Marty's ever done is help people. Her gift—her pass, if you will, for all that selflessness she's displayed—as far as I'm concerned, is immortality."

She wanted to crawl under a rock when she was done. She'd known she'd come off all gushy fangirl, but there was no other way to explain how unjust this mess was.

Nina dragged a hand through her hair before cracking her knuckles. "She's one badass bitch. I tease her all the damn time, but she's braver and smarter than I'll ever be."

As if she hadn't heard all the stories... "Still another reason her immortality should count for something."

Scratching at Dwayne Johnson's ears, Nina dropped one of Rocky's worst fears into the conversation. "You've probably already thought about this, but I'm gonna say it any fucking way. Her being on this list... This could also mean someone *wants* our girl dead. It's not like we haven't fucked up someone's day a time or two."

Rocky shivered. All through the amazing dinner of roast leg of lamb with a divine mint/garlic sauce and fingerling potatoes so tender they'd make your mother weep, as she'd let the candied baby carrots melt in her mouth, she'd wondered the same thing.

She ran her fingers along Muffin's spine, and as the dog sighed in contentment, shook her head.

"That's one of the conclusions I've toyed with. Someone wants Marty out of the picture and they put her name on that list. Which leaves us with the fact you guys have some powerful, scary enemies."

Nina barked a soft laugh, the sound dripping scorn. "You don't do what we do without making fucking enemies, but I can't think of any with a specific grudge against Marty. If anything, they'd want *me* dead. I am the loudest-mouth bitch in our little trio from hell."

All night long, Nina had lived up to her legendary reputation, but the trait Rocky admired the most was her honesty. She knew her faults and she freely admitted they existed, but that she didn't care only made her more real to Rocky.

Running the heel of her hand over her eyes, she fought a yawn. She'd been running on empty for two days now while they'd prepared to bring Marty home, fretting over what to do and how to approach them, and it was beginning to show.

"I don't know who it could be if it's not someone who has beef with you guys, but I need you all to think hard on it. Think about all the cases you've been on, the people you've helped, longtime grudges, whatever. I'll need some hardcore proof to present to my superiors to prevent them from intervening and taking her soul anyway."

Nina's face turned hard as she clenched a fist and straightened her spine. "Just let a motherfucker come. I'll make sure he doesn't walk for a flippin' month."

Rocky couldn't help but giggle, but she had to make Nina understand, brute force wouldn't cut it. "You can't stop a reap, Nina. No one but another reaper can. We control souls almost like puppet masters. The saying about when your time is up is really true. It really is up."

Hudson poked his handsome head outside Marty's sprawling bedroom and smiled his ruggedly handsome smile. "Everything looks good if you want to sit and visit for a bit, Nina."

Nina rose on long legs after giving Dwayne Johnson one last scratch and dropping a kiss on the top of his head. "Don't go anywhere, Reaper. I'm not done by a longshot. I have more questions, but I'll be back after I croon my favorite Barry Manilow tune to my girl in there. She hates when I sing to her. Maybe that'll wake her ass up." Then she cackled, her long hair spilling over her shoulders.

Rocky patted her backpack with her clothes, having opted to sleep on the floor outside Marty's room rather than have a room to herself. At this point, she wasn't willing to leave her in anyone else's hands but her own.

"I'm not going anywhere. I'll be right here on the couch, sleeping with one eye open and my trusty scythe."

Rocky spread a hand out to encompass the sitting room with its lush couch in oyster white, a TV longer than a railway car, and cozy knit throws in turquoise and pops of royal blue.

Nina pointed a finger at her and gave her a stern look, but there was a twinkle in her eye. "You be sure you do that."

"Aye-aye, Captain," Rocky acknowledged, rising herself to kick off her shoes and put them neatly in the corner.

Nina began to whistle "Don't Fear The Reaper" as she made her way into Marty's room.

"Very original, vampire! As if I haven't heard that a hundred times before!"

Hudson ventured farther into the room, passing a

laughing Nina. He eyed Rocky for a moment before he asked, "Mind if I sit for a little while?"

She shrugged, hoping to keep her attitude of indifference in check. She had to keep the wall between them in place. "It's a free country."

But he just kept right on smiling, dropping down on the couch and patting it to invite Muffin to sit with him. As she hopped up and curled into his lap, he asked, "So you're really a reaper?"

Looking anywhere but directly at him, Rocky nodded, sitting on the other end of the fluffy couch. "I'm the real deal. Spooky, Gothic robe, death and all."

"Interesting line of work."

"Reaping? Taking lives as opposed to your saving them?"

If it were possible, he grinned harder, his eyes twinkling, but he'd clearly picked up on her defensive tone. "Easy there. I'm just trying to make friends. We're all in this together."

She leaned into the back of the couch, crossing her leg over her knee, and said casually, "I have plenty of friends. I'm not here to make friends. I'm here to protect Marty from the reap."

"Okey-doke then. No friends for Rocky. Friendship is absolutely off the table. Do not make friends with the reaper," he teased, sending a ripple of irritation along her spine.

She couldn't be his friend. It wasn't allowed. Not only because of her superiors but because of her heart.

Yet, looking at his face, so open and totally unaware of their past experiences on the In Between, guilt poked at her guts. He didn't know why she harbored some resentment. It wasn't his fault he didn't remember her, and in the interest of keeping the peace for all concerned and not causing a ruckus, she decided she could be a little friendly.

But only a little.

With a sigh, Rocky leaned farther into the cushions on the couch. "Look, I don't mean to come off so harsh. I'm just focused on doing what needs to be done. I don't have the kinds of abilities these women do. Aside from my scythe, all I have is my big mouth and reason on my side. If they ever show up, it's going to take a lot of fancy footwork to convince my superiors that this is a mistake."

He nodded in understanding, his dark eyes going soft. "Listen, no one gets red tape better than me. You do remember Dr. Valentine is my superior, don't you?"

She let out a small chuckle. "Yeah, he's kind of a bag of dicks. A fair point if there ever was one, indeed."

"So can you be fired for doing this? Do reapers get the boot for misconduct?"

"No, but we can go to reaper jail for disobedience." And she'd heard it was a none-too friendly place with tighter security than Fort Knox. "I think refusing to collect a soul classifies as willful disobedience at its finest."

He sat up, the muscles in his arms rippling beneath his dark green cable-knit sweater as he repositioned himself on the couch to face her, and she had to look down at her hands to forget those arms had once held her.

"So you're risking going to jail to keep Marty's soul intact?"

Okay, when Hudson said it out loud, it sounded a little outlandish and maybe even a little extra, but yeah. That was the gist.

"I'm just trying to do the right thing," she whispered, her heart contracting before she steeled herself against the memory of their intimate conversation so long ago.

His eyes gleamed under the soft lighting. "Look, I know nothing about reaping, but I have to hand it to you for taking this to the next level. It's pretty brave."

Dwayne Johnson lifted his head and grumbled in his sleep before rolling over and resting his head on her foot.

Rocky shrugged. "It's not totally selfless. If I'm honest, I don't want the bad press and backlash for taking an immortal as famous as Marty. Do you have any idea what paranormal Twitter is like? They'd eat me alive. There'd be ugly hashtags and trending topics with me as the star punching bag. This is self-preservation from her rabid fans."

He barked a laugh, then covered his mouth with his wrist and shook his head. "I'm not much for social media, but that you came here and had the guts to tell these women, especially Nina, says a lot about your character and your moral compass."

Enough about her and bravery. Talk like that made her uncomfortable. She did what she did. He didn't need to know her personal reasons for doing it.

"So what made you decide to take this job? It couldn't have been easy to arrange to leave the hospital. Did Dr. Valentine pitch the fit of all fits?"

As they'd eaten dinner, and she'd heard bits and pieces of the offer the ladies and their husbands had made to Hudson, but she didn't understand why he'd taken the bait. He had a solid job at the hospital, why would he leave and risk losing it? Money, maybe?

He shrugged, his eyes taking on a distant look as he

stroked Muffin's back. "I guess I'm just impressed with how determined they are to see their friend through this. They're loyal as hell. How often do you see that kind of loyalty?"

"As a phoenix who's seen many lives, I'd think you've seen it quite often."

He cocked his head, his eyes instantly sharp. "How did you know I was a phoenix?"

Yeah. How did you know that, Rocky?

But she just shrugged despite the two red spots on her cheeks and kept things vague. "It's not a secret, is it? I think I heard one of the housekeeping staff talk about it. I can't really remember."

"I don't know if I can really fully explain what made me take this job. It just felt important, and over the month Marty's been in my care, I've come to like these people."

"Even Nina?" she couldn't help but ask with an impish grin. "Does anyone really like Nina?"

"Why am I hearing my name, Reaper?" Nina crowed.

"Rocky was just remarking on how hard it is to believe anyone likes you, Nina, but I assured her, I like you best of all," he said, shooting her a mischievous grin then setting Muffin on the couch and hopping upward.

"Way to throw me under the bus, Hudson" she drawled at him, tinting her voice with as much sarcasm as she could muster.

He grinned on a chuckle, a deep, delicious, husky chuckle that sent shivers along her arms. "I aim to please. Now, I'm going to go check on my patient one last time before bed. Oh, and don't think I've forgotten this. I still say I know you from *somewhere*, Rocky."

"No you do not!" she singsonged, trying to keep a

teasing tone to her voice, even though a bit of panic was beginning to set in. "In what world would a lowly janitor like me know a fancy, rich, Mercedes-driving cardiologist like you?"

He chuckled again as he made his way into the bedroom, the sound settling in her ears, a sound she found all too pleasant—a sound that left her belly warm and her heart skipping beats.

But then she looked up at Nina, glaring down at her with a question written all over her gorgeously flawless face, and she sat up straight, clearing her throat.

Nina frowned and gave Rocky's leg a shove as she sat down on the couch, before leaning forward and scooping up Dwayne Johnson, cuddling him on her lap.

As she cupped his bulky chin and he grunted at her, she smiled and cooed, "Tell your Flirty McFlirt mommy now's not the time to start a bad romance. We have shit to figure out and it fucking doesn't involve kissy-face."

Rocky couldn't help but laugh as she snuggled into the couch, pulling a pillow to her jittery stomach to tamp down her fears.

The long hours of the night worried her most. It was probably the time a reaper would most likely appear. It was oftentimes easier on the reaper to take a soul if they didn't have to witness sorrow-filled family and friends, grieving over a loved one. This job was hard enough as it was—even when the soul was ready.

Still, there were some souls that broke your heart into a million pieces; even the most hardened reaper would tell you that. The children. Those who had suffered, be it from disease or life's cruelties and injustice. Minimal emotions surrounding the body always made the reap less difficult. A reaper would avoid them as often as possible.

So, as she listened to Nina list some possible suspects from their past battles with half an ear, she also listened for the distinctly low hum of the reap.

And held her breath.

And prayed.

CHAPTER 6

"*M*istress Rocky, might I offer you more cheesy eggs?" Archibald asked, his smile warm across the long table where they all sat, finishing up breakfast for dinner.

Rocky ran a hand over her stomach and shook her head with her impish smile—one Hudson found he was growing fonder of by the second, even if she gave him the cold shoulder at every opportunity.

"You've cheesy-egged me into a food coma—" She stopped short, realizing her insensitivity, he guessed. Her eyes went instantly to the women as she nibbled at her lower lip. "Oh, hell... I'm so sorry—"

But Nina only cackled as she bounced Wanda's baby, Sam, on her knee, his lightly tinted green face wreathed in a gummy smile. "Don't be stupid, Reaper. Marty'd damn well laugh her ass off. She uses that expression with Arch all the time."

Keegan half-smiled, even if it was only for a brief

moment before his eyes clouded back over. "Nina's right. She wouldn't want you walking on eggshells."

Blowing out a breath, her chest rising and falling, Rocky tucked a lock of her long chestnut hair behind her ear, so shiny, so soft, Hudson wanted to thread his fingers through the silky strands. "Okay," she whispered, still clearly unsure.

Wanda reached out a finely boned hand and squeezed Rocky's arm with a chuckle. "No, really. She'd definitely get a kick out of this. And when she wakes up, and we tell her everything she's put us through, she'll laugh even harder."

Darnell, a big linebacker of a man in jeans, a football jersey and high-tops seated next to Rocky, wrapped an arm around her shoulders, giving her a light squeeze. "She's tellin' ya true, Rocky. I can't wait for you ta meet our girl. You'll see. She's got a sense a humor. Yep, she does."

Carl, who sat on the other side of her, thumped her hand with his duct-taped fingers and nodded, his sweet, open face genuine. "Yes. Thhh...the..." He paused, pursing his lips. "Truuuth."

Carl had really developed a thing for Rocky. He sat with her outside Marty's room as often as possible, his eyes moony and round, and today, he'd brought her a bouquet of broccoli, making Hudson's chest tighten.

Rocky patted him on the arm and smiled warmly, flashing her white teeth as she pushed out her chair. "Thanks, Carl. Come upstairs later and we'll read together, okay? For now, I'd better get up there. And thanks for an amazing dinner, Arch. You're one of the best parts of my day."

Arch nodded his head, the tuft of hair atop his balding skull bouncing in unison. "You are always welcome at my table, Mistress Rocky. I hope you saved room for some cake. I made a delightful German chocolate. Extra coconut because I heard a rumor you're rather fond of it."

Rocky went around the table to Arch's side and gave him a quick hug. "You really are the best thing that's ever happened to my palette."

He barked a laugh and cupped her chin before she turned to leave the dining room and head toward her post.

They'd been together in Marty and Keegan's beautiful home for two days straight now, all of them doing what they did on a mostly normal basis. They'd eaten meals in Marty's room with her, they played games with the children, they read to her, and in general tried to go on doing what they might do if the circumstances were normal.

Keegan's sister Mara, and his brother Sloan, and their respective spouses had shown up, too. Everyone had skin in the game. They were all deeply invested in Marty waking up.

Yet still, nothing. Marty's vitals remained the same, strong and steady, and so did her status as un-reaped. But no one had shown up to collect her soul. In fact, there seemed to be no inkling anyone on the reaper side even knew her soul was still alive and well.

All the while, he'd tried to get to know Rocky, as resistant to the idea as she appeared. That niggling feeling in the back of his brain that just wouldn't let him rest said they knew each other.

Spending time with her to try to discover their origins felt like the thing to do. So he hung around the fringes of her presence as much as possible when his responsibility to Marty didn't take him away.

And yeah. She was short with him. Sometimes she even outright ignored him. But every time he thought he'd let this nagging feeling be, because he wasn't into forcing himself on anyone, especially a woman, she'd smile or laugh at one of his jokes and he was sucked in all over again.

Today she looked exhausted, and as they excused themselves and left the table to head up the stairs, her for another long shift of watching out for shadows in the night, and him to check her fluids and stats, it showed in her weary footsteps.

"I can't believe I said that," she muttered, rolling up the sleeves of her sweatshirt when they hit the top of the stairs and made a hard right toward the sitting room.

Her dedication to this, her heart, drew him to her like a moth to a flame. A life spent with so few attachments, even immortal ones, always made him wish for dinners like the one they had every night with the OOPS gang.

Unfortunately, his lifespan was typically five hundred years, which, sure, seems like a long time—until you die, reincarnate, and forget almost every single person and possession you had. It meant starting all over again every damn time. And he always started a new life fully grown—a fully grown adult with amnesia.

Not total amnesia. He always remembered where he lived and the occasional face. But enough that it made it hard to revisit anyone and expect the other party to walk you through your life and help you relearn things like how to use a cell phone or call an Uber.

So he'd made an effort not to become too attached since as far back as he could remember. An inconvenience was the last thing he wanted to become to anyone.

Refocusing on Rocky so as not to dwell, Hudson stopped for a moment and touched her arm. "I think they made it clear Marty would find it funny," he reassured, gazing down at her worried face, so beautiful with the light sprinkle of freckles over her nose. "Don't fret."

Her round eyes clouded as she twisted her fingers. "Is it funny to use a word like that when Marty's like this?" She pointed to the interior of the bedroom, where Marty still lie hooked up to machines, fresh from the sponge bath Keegan had so tenderly given her, all while he told her how much he loved her. "I think not. It was insensitive and rude, after they've all been so kind to me when I showed up on their doorstep unannounced and declared myself some kind of guardian angel. Which I'm most definitely not. In fact, I'm the exact opposite."

He sensed she was overwhelmed. Not just in her tone or her words, but her body language, which he'd swear on his next five lives, he knew.

"Hey." He tapped her lightly on the shoulder as she took her place on the sitting room couch, her standard modus operandi these past couple of days as she sat watch. "I think you're forgetting something here. You're doing them a favor, too, Rocky. You've been in this sitting room for two days with only snippets of sleep, looking out for their friend. You're anything but insensitive. You don't even know these people. Yet here you are, staying up all night long to watch over Marty."

She waved him off with the wrinkle of her nose and settled into the couch, snapping her fingers to show Dwayne Johnson he should follow. "Just because you're doing something kind, that doesn't give someone a pass to be insensitive. What I said was insensitive."

As Dwayne hopped onto the couch, burrowing under one of the knit throws against her leg, Hudson sat down, too, facing Rocky. "And you apologized. The end. Now, you really need to get some sleep. You're exhausted. Why not lie down and I'll take a shift?"

Pulling a throw around her legs, she rubbed Dwayne Johnson's ears, making him hum his approval with a snort. "A, because you're her doctor and you have other things to worry about, like keeping Marty alive and stable. B, because you won't hear the sound of the reap."

He cocked his head and frowned, running a hand over his stubble-covered jaw. "You can *hear* the sound of a reaper?" Man, you learned something new every day.

Just when he thought she was coming out of her shell, she retreated, her lips stiff and tight when she said, "*I* can. *You* can't."

"So you really are the only one who can do this."

"That's correct. Not that I'd trust anyone else anyway. There aren't many rule-breakers like me. Reapers are all a bunch of sheeple who do the cosmos's bidding without question. So I kept my mouth shut about my intentions with Marty. Only one person knows where I am right now, and I hope to keep it that way."

"I hear a lot of bitter in your tone."

Rocky sighed. "You heard right, I guess. Not everyone's an exception to the rule. If a reaper didn't take the souls he or she was assigned strictly based on our tender *feelings*, we'd have more than an overpopulation problem. But I'll never understand why no one's ever questioned a reap before me. We just blindly reap."

"Ahhh," he drawled. She really was the reaper with a heart. "So you've done this before? Questioned a reap?"

Rocky made a face, pushing her hair from her flashing eyes. "Not to this degree, but I have questioned the sanity of a reap or two, and you know what I got back? *There has to be a balance of good and evil, Rocky. That's just the way it goes. The universe unfolds the way it was meant to unfold,*" she mimicked in a smug tone. "I'm not sure why the universe can't be filled with only good, but I guess people have to have something to fight for, right? A purpose, a reason to get up in the morning. But Marty's reap isn't just about my feelings, Hudson. It's just wrong. It's damn well *wrong*, and I'm tired of shutting up and following some unknown, faceless leader. I've been doing it for too long, and it's time to take a stand."

He smiled at her grit, putting his arm on the back of the couch and letting his head rest on his hand. Then he wondered something out loud. "Reapers are immortal, right? But I haven't seen any at the hospitals I've worked at in all my lifetimes. That I remember, anyway."

She fought a yawn, pressing her fingers to her luscious lips. "As the day is long. We're usually a hearty bunch as far as I know, but if you're wondering whether we can be killed, slicing our heads off is the only way."

Hudson winced at her and rubbed his neck. "Ouch."

Pulling the throw up under her chin, she half-closed her eyes and said, "But it's only happened once in the history of reapers, and it was, according to urban legend, a total accident."

Cocking his head, he gave her a strange look. "How do you *accidentally* slice off someone's head?"

With a gurgle of laughter, Rocky grinned. "A reaper was collecting a soul in like medieval times or something, and he accidentally tripped some kind of a wire trap the guy whose soul he was collecting had set for his enemies. Sliced his head clean off." She dragged a finger across her throat for effect.

Hudson whistled, giving Dwayne Johnson a scratch on his rounded belly. "Double ouch." He paused for a moment while he watched her dark eyelashes flutter over her cheeks. "So, you've been reaping for a while?"

"Centuries," she offered dully.

"Ah. So you're a senior citizen. You look good for your age."

"I could say the same about you."

"That I look good for my age?" he teased with a wink. "I try. I work out, I try to eat right. Though with these delicious meals Arch keeps making, I'm pretty sure I'm going to need a diet when I go home."

"No," she said, deadpan. "I meant that you're a senior citizen, too."

He laughed, watching the rise and fall of her chest as she settled in. "Look who suddenly got a sense of humor."

She hunkered down under the throw and sighed, her face going blank. "My job doesn't exactly encourage a lot of laughter. I try to find some where I can."

"Yeah," he said on a sigh, tucking the blanket around her ankles. "Sometimes—I take that back—a lot of times, mine doesn't either. I get it. Ever considered switching jobs?"

Turning to her side, she tucked a hand under her cheek.

"I didn't choose the reap, the reap chose me. I was born into it centuries ago—it's my legacy. I don't have a choice."

Rocky appeared to be engaging him without that disapproving look she'd shot at him since they'd met, so he decided to ask more questions in the hopes she'd open up.

"So like me, you've lived through a lot of eras in history. What's been your favorite so far?"

She smiled in dreamy fashion. "Believe it or not, the '80s. Well, maybe it's a tie between that and the Victorian era. Oh, those dresses. I loved them—even those stupid corsets and bustles—but the hats were divine. But mostly I'm a Lisa-Lisa and the Cult Jam, Prince kind of girl. I miss the hair the most, though. Who doesn't want big metal hair?" she asked sleepily.

"Or to be able to use gag me with a spoon in a sentence?" he joked.

"So what about you? What's your favorite era? As a phoenix, you've lived through a few, I imagine."

He shrugged his shoulders and sucked in his cheeks. "While yes, I've lived a bunch of lives, I don't know because I mostly don't remember them. I die at five hundred years old, rise from the ashes and begin all over again. I even have to study to become a doctor all over again, but somehow, that's the profession that always speaks to me."

If only people knew the kind of hell taking the MCATS could be. But it was what he loved—it was in his blood.

Rocky was silent for a moment, as though she had to digest that before she said, "Wow. That's rough. Is it a surprise when you find out you're the only living phoenix?"

"Now, there's the strange thing about my entire existence. The only reason I know I'm a phoenix is because I can shift. That happens as I reincarnate. You know, wings, beak, squawking, the whole nine. Somehow, that part of me always knows what to do and that I have to be careful around humans in the event of discovery, which is why I chose to go into medicine for the paranormal—because I don't have to explain why I don't look a day over thirty-five."

"Ya think? I'd have said forty, but whatever," she teased.

"And I always come back with this," he said, pulling the gold necklace he reincarnated with from under his sweater to show her.

Rocky stared at it for a minute as he ran a finger over the charm, a small cross—one he never failed to have around his neck after rebirth, but never understood why. And the people who knew him after he was reborn didn't seem to know either.

She then looked at him for what felt like forever, her blue eyes, once half-closed, now wide open before they softened ever so slightly. "That must be really hard on you, with no family or friends. I mean, my father's a total hardass, a by-the-reaper-book kind of guy, but I love him. I can count on him...mostly. I don't know what I'd do if I was reborn every five hundred years and I didn't have him to come back to."

He heard the sympathy in her voice and looked away, staring at the television's blank screen to avoid getting too deep into his feelings. He didn't want to scare her off, but encourage her to see he was a decent enough guy.

"Your dad's a hardass? You don't get along?"

Rocky's pretty peachy lips thinned. "Next subject. Answer the question."

He played dumb. "What was the question?"

"Is it hard doing life alone without any family?"

He hadn't realized just *how* hard until this lot came into his life. But in the interest of allowing more people into his life because it felt so good, he decided to answer honestly.

"Sometimes. But I get by. I have a job I love. Patients I love."

"And?" she coaxed with a gentle grin.

"And what?"

"What else do you have besides your job, Hudson? Pets? Hobbies?"

He ran his hand over Dwayne Johnson's back. "No pets, but I love animals. Thought about becoming a vet, but doing that in the human world would raise a lot of questions about my longevity, if you know what I mean. Also, I work a lot. I wouldn't want to leave a dog for fourteen hours at a time while I scrub in on a heart surgery."

Rocky smiled at him. "You favor dogs over cats?"

"I like 'em all, but I'd really love a dog of my own someday."

"So your hobbies..." she encouraged.

He didn't have time for many hobbies under the iron rule of Dr. Valentine, but he had a couple he indulged in when he had time off. "I like to read. I play a mean game of golf. Though, I don't get a lot of time off. Dr. Valentine is a demanding taskmaster."

"Are you part of a book club? Golf club? Any club?"

He furrowed his brow. "Do they have golf clubs?"

"They have clubs for everything from hangnails to bad hair days. I'm sure they do."

"Are *you* part of any clubs?"

"We're not talking about me, we're talking about you," she deflected, closing her eyes again and stretching her toes. "So are you part of any clubs?"

"No, but hearing about this bad hair day club could possibly sway me into joining one. Who doesn't want a safe place to air their grief about a bad hair?" he joked, finally getting a chance to really look at her without interruption and see if it jogged his memory.

She giggled at his answer. "Well, maybe you should. You could...make some..."

She drifted off quite suddenly then, taking a tiny sip of air before her breathing grew even and she was fast asleep.

But Hudson smiled. Like *really* smiled.

This was the first time she'd actually willingly engaged in conversation with him and even though she was contrary at times, he liked that, too.

Still, he almost physically felt that wall she had up, and he didn't understand the reason for it.

But he'd like to break it down.

He'd really like that.

CHAPTER 7

*T*he loud hiss of a machine woke Rocky from a sound sleep. It almost sounded like a balloon, popping off the top of a tank of helium.

Hoping she'd been dreaming, she jolted upward, falling off the couch in the sitting room and nearly tripping over Dwayne Johnson, who'd apparently forgotten he was a dog who should bark at strange noises.

But there is was again. *Hiss, hiss, hisssss.*

Bleary-eyed and exhausted, she wanted to kick herself for falling asleep. Why had Hudson let her fall asleep when she'd told him she was the only person who could hear a reaper?

And for the love of pineapples, what the hell was that damn hissing noise?

Without thinking, Rocky followed her ears, tiptoeing into Marty's room where the sound grew, reverberating around the space. She hadn't been in here, only on the fringes in order to respect the privacy of the ladies, their husbands and, most of all, Marty.

89

She didn't want to appear as though she were gawking or interfering in anyway, so she didn't know the entire lay of the land.

The curtains had been drawn over the large floor-to-ceiling windows, and there was nothing but the light of the heart monitor and a small night-light illuminating the room. She could see Marty's frame, covered in a bulky comforter; what she guessed was a large armoire across the room from the bed; and two oval-shaped pieces of furniture on either side of the bed, which she assumed were night-stands. But they were all just outlines at this point.

Making her way deeper into the room, Rocky held her breath as she squinted into the dark, and the hissing grew louder—

And that's when she saw the hulking figure by the bed.

A brick wall of an ominous shadow popped up, and the flash of a white tube sent the blood in Rocky's veins ice cold.

Marty's breathing tube had been pulled out—that was the hissing sound!

Panic rocketed to her belly, making her break out into a cold sweat.

Whoever this was—and for sure it was no reaper—had pulled Marty's breathing tube from her throat. Why would anyone...

And then an explanatory word tore through the layers of sleep and shock—a heinous, ugly word.

Murder? Someone was trying to kill Marty?

Without thinking, without even considering the fact that her scythe was in the sitting room or that she had no real physical power, Rocky launched herself across the room and lunged for the shadowy figure.

"*Noooo!*" she screamed, aiming for his middle section as her head connected to the solid wall of his torso. But she managed to at least knock him down, making him drop the breathing tube, for all the good that would do.

As her eyes adjusted further, he scooped her up off the floor, lifting her high over his head, she realized he was covered head to toe in black and wearing a facemask, just before he threw her against the wall.

He roared his anguish, a roar so fierce, so rattling, it shook the whole room. Just before impact, the chandelier above Marty's bed rocked and chimed.

Hitting the wall didn't just hurt. Rocky was convinced it shattered every bone in her body as she crumbled with a yelp before falling to the floor, knocking the wind out of her.

That was when she tried to cry out for help, but her ribs hurt so much she couldn't breathe.

Mere seconds later, a blinding white light screamed into the room.

On instinct, Rocky tried to raise a hand to cover her eyes, but the loud screech that followed the light ripped through her ears.

And then she saw him in all his magnificently winged glory.

Hudson in phoenix form.

The wind he created when he flapped his wings was so ferocious, it pinned her against the wall where she'd fallen, the squawk of his cry deafening. In the blink of an eye, he was running toward the shadowy figure, scarlet-and-gold-feathered head down, moving at the speed of light.

He crashed into the intruder, driving his beak into his stomach, knocking him so hard, Rocky heard him grunt before the glass of the window shattered, sending shards and splinters raining down to the tune of his scream as he fell.

She fought to scramble to her feet, knowing Marty needed that tube to keep breathing. Panic rushed through her in a wave of fear and pain. The throb racking her body as she hauled herself upward nearly took her breath away, but she managed to get herself to the edge of Marty's king-size bed and pull herself up, her fingers digging into the side of the mattress.

Trying to keep her head on straight as she tore her way to the surface of the bed, she realized she didn't know anything about breathing tubes, but she did know CPR.

"What in all of the entirety of fuck is going on?" Nina hollered into the room as she stormed in, her hair wild and flying behind her as the wind whooshed in, her eyes blazing and fiery.

"The window," Rocky squeaked, fighting the searing fire in her ribs as the heart monitor flatlined with a screech. "He went out the window with Hudson behind him. Help Hudson!" She pointed to the broken glass as the infernal hiss of the damn tube continued.

Nina didn't spare a second before she yelled an order to Wanda, "Help Rocky!" and launched herself out the window, too.

Hands were reaching for her, hands that tried to be gentle but hurt like hell. Yet, she pushed them away as she leaned forward, pinching Marty's nose and placing her mouth over hers. All she could remember was if the heart had stopped, it was two breaths and thirty compressions.

Just as she was about to breath into Marty's mouth, she heard Hudson's soothing voice, somewhere far off in the muddled distance, and felt a hand on her shoulder. "Rocky. Stop. It's okay. I've got this now."

Someone else lifted her off the bed, away from Marty. Someone big and soft, who tucked her into their arms and carried her out of the bedroom and down a long hallway.

Her head pounded so hard, her ribs searing with white-hot pain as she was placed on a surface that felt like a cloud. There were orders barked and frantic footsteps sounded right before she passed out.

~

"Kiddo? Open your eyes."

"Hmmm," she groaned. It was comfortable where she was. Quiet. Why would she open her eyes? It was the most sleep she'd had in days.

A knuckle trailed its way down along her cheek with a gentle pass. "Reeeeaper, Aunty Nina says it's time to get up. No more falling down on the fucking job, lazy ass."

She felt a nudge to her leg then the bed sank beside her. "Caaarl sayyy soo…oo, too."

Rocky smiled. Sweet Carl. He was gentle and kind and even if his body parts fell off all the time, he'd brought her a broccoli bouquet. According to Nina, they were the quintessential gift from Carl.

As she fought her way through the haze of unconsciousness, the earlier events came rushing back to her, sending her into a panic.

"Marty?" she croaked, her fingers clenching the sheets to try to pull herself up.

But Nina placed a flat palm on her shoulder and lightly squeezed. "She's fine. Birdman fixed her right up. Tube's back in and she's breathing. You, on the other hand, are a fucked-up mess. But nice stab at kicking a guy's ass. I'm impressed you're not *more* fucked up."

The other side of the bed sank beside her, and she heard, "Birdman here. Can you open your eyes for me, Rocky?"

Hearing Hudson's voice made her eyes pop wide open, and then the rush of his scent, his sound, flooded her senses.

She was in a room painted in a navy blue with white accents on a bed made of clouds, and sheets so soft, they felt like newborn baby skin.

Rocky stared up at him, catching Carl's worried gaze from the corner of her eye. She squeezed his hand and shot him a weak smile. "I'm fine, Carl. Promise."

Hudson put two fingers on her temples and pulled her eyelids up, shining a light into them and making her cringe. "Looks good. Now, tell me where it hurts."

"Maybe I should tell you where it doesn't hurt. I think the nail of my left pinkie qualifies."

When he let her eyelids go with a bark of laughter, she realized he was naked from the waist up. Her eyes flew to his chest, and then to his face wreathed in a smile. "The shift. I always lose my damn shirt. I can't tell you how often I have to buy new work shirts," he explained.

If only his chest weren't so tan, so rippled, with a sprinkling of dark hair between his pecs, maybe she could focus on something else, like the dull ache in her ribs and the throb of her eyeball. But it was damn hard with the kind of confidence he exuded.

She sure as hell wouldn't sit around with no shirt on in front of a bunch of people she barely knew.

"You have a real shiner there, but your ribs feel okay. How would you feel about letting me take you to the hospital for some X-rays, just to be sure?" he asked, leaning over her to reposition her pillows, allowing his all-male scent to linger in her nose.

Rocky shook her head and attempted to sit up. "No hospital. If I never go back there again, it'll be too soon. Not a fan. Besides, I really feel okay. Just bruised and a little battered."

Hudson gave her his doctor-ly look. "I thought you might say that…and it's a deal, but if you have any trouble at all breathing, or you feel dizzy, lightheaded, you'd better speak up, or I'm throwing you over my shoulder and taking you there myself."

She shivered, but nodded her agreement. "So, let's talk about what just happened. First, you let me fall asleep! Why would you do that?"

Hudson gave her a guilty look, his eyes flooded with concern. "I fell asleep, too. I'm sorry, Rocky. I wasn't even that tired, but it just sort of happened without me realizing it. I woke up to the sound of you screaming and…you know the rest."

Sighing, she touched her fiery face with a tentative finger. "That's fair. It's not your job to keep me awake."

Nina crossed her feet at the ankles—feet clad in red thermal footie pajamas. "We need to figure out a better system than this, kiddo. You can't stay awake until she fucking wakes up, waiting on a reaper who might never show. Who knows how long it'll be before she opens her damn eyes."

Also fair, but the only way to do that was to invite another reaper in, and she couldn't think of any other reaper who'd rebel against the system.

"We'll talk about that later. For now, there's this: That was no reaper, Nina. I know the scent of a reaper. I know the feel of another reaper. Any ideas on who the hell that was?" Then she remembered Nina and Hudson had flown out the window after the intruder. "Did you see who it was, Nina? Hudson?"

Calamity, who she hadn't seen since she'd arrived, hopped up on the bed, her tail swishing in the air. "It was magic."

Rocky cocked her head, pushing away Hudson's hands and sitting up anyway. "Magic? What are you talking about? Is that a person?"

Calamity shook her tiny dark head and rubbed up against Rocky's leg with a purr. "Not a person. A thing."

Nina sat down on the bed just as Wanda flew into the room in her blue fuzzy bathrobe and matching slippers, still light on her feet for being so pregnant. "Rocky! Oh heavens, are you all right?" she asked, her tired eyes worried as she reached for Rocky's hand, tucking it into her soft one.

"I'm fine. Just sore. Calamity was just telling me this attack on Marty had to do with magic? I don't get it."

Nina popped her lips. "Not sure if you knew this, but I'm half witch. Long story about how the fuck *that* happened, but it's true. Calamity's my familiar—or did you know that?

Never mind, doesn't fucking matter. Anyway, I can smell fucking magic because of my ability to track with my vampire senses, and for sure, it was magic. I smelled the spell. I don't know what the fuck kind or why, but there was magic involved."

"Fuck all if it's not the strangest thing, too. She sucks at spells, but she can smell 'em from a hundred miles away," Calamity groused.

Rocky was confused, and she guessed her expression said as much. "I'm not pickin' up what you're layin' down. How can magic and a spell be the responsible party? It didn't look like magic to me. He yanked her breathing tube out. That's attempted murder. There's nothing magical about it."

Wanda tugged a length of Rocky's hair and smiled down at her. "What Nina means is, the person who tried to kill Marty was, we think, under the influence of magic."

Fear swept over Rocky, making her unable to fight a shiver. Whoa. That was a whole other ball of wax. She didn't know anything about magic. "So now we don't just have a reaper to worry about, but some unknown murderer?"

Nina tweaked her cheek and grinned. "Smart reaper is smart," she joked. "Yep. That's still true, but we do know who fucking pulled her breathing tube out."

"You mean the person you *think* was under the influence of magic," Rocky said, in a wooden tone. "But you don't know for sure if you're right?"

Nina's brow furrowed and her eyes flashed as though Rocky were crazy to doubt her. "I'm almost one hundred."

Her mouth fell open, and it took her a moment to gather

her words. "Almost. but you're not one hundred. In the meantime, why aren't you stringing him up by his balls with dental floss from one of Marty's trees until you know for sure? *Who are you?* You nearly knocked my face off when I just rang the doorbell. Someone tries to murder Marty and you're all *here*, babying *me*? Why aren't you pounding his head in right this second? Yanking his innards through his nose? Doing all those things you guys threaten on the reg?"

"Because he's just outside in the other room having tea with Archibald and Darnell and he seems pretty legit," Hudson said, giving Harry—Mara's husband, who'd appeared in the doorway—a grateful smile when he handed him a T-shirt.

Now she became afraid. These people were imposters. Like pod people or something. No way in all of the universe would they allow the person who'd possibly tried to murder Marty have a spot of tea and some cookies.

Backing away, she scooted forward across the surface of the bed, forgetting her ribs felt like arrows of fire and her eyeball might surely pop out of her head if she moved it too much.

Raising a finger, she turned and shouted, "*Who are you?*" When Nina made a move toward her, Rocky whipped up a hand to thwart her, aghast. "Stay back! Don't you come any closer or I swear, I'll...I'll..." She shook her head, making her face throb. "I don't know what I'll do, but I'll do it, and even if you kill me, it won't be without a fight! You're not the Wanda and Nina I know. The Wanda and Nina I know wouldn't serve tea to a man unless they know for certain he didn't try and murder their friend!"

Mara, Marty's sister-in-law, and the woman named

Jeannie, who was married to Marty's brother-in-law, Sloan, pushed their way into the bedroom.

She tucked her incredibly shiny black hair behind her ears. "What are you doing to this poor thing, Nna? You're going to wake the kids! Sam's having the worst night teething while you're in here fooling around. Knock it off," Mara said, planting her hands on her slender hips.

Jeannie, a petite, pretty lady with a high ponytail, looked to Mara. "Did you threaten someone's insides again, Nina? I thought all that therapy and anger management fixed you." And then she giggled.

"Why the fuck is it always my goddamned fault?" Nina crowed.

Jeannie puffed her chest out, pounding it with two fists. "Because when there's noise and chaos involved, it usually is."

"Hey, fuck you and your noise, I Dream of," Nina said, giving Jeannie the finger.

Hudson and Harry both burst out laughing.

"Why is this so funny?" Rocky yelped.

Wanda gave her a smile of sympathy and finally said, "Because when you see who the person in the other room is, you'll understand why we believe he had no control over his actions. He was under a spell, honey. We're pretty sure it was some kind of controlling spell."

Oh.

She relaxed a little, but only a little. She wasn't going to let her guard entirely down until she asked some questions. "So who is this person who tried to kill Marty?"

Hudson smoothed a hand over his T-shirt before his gorgeous gaze met hers. "You'll never believe it."

Rocky narrowed her eyes, reaching for the silver night-stand beside the bed to help hold her up. "Because everything else you've all been telling me makes complete sense? Just tell me who it is."

Hudson's eyes were amused and he snickered as though he were keeping some secret. Then he said, "It's Dr. Doomsday. Er, I mean, Dr. Valentine. Dr. Valentine tried to kill Marty."

CHAPTER 8

"I still don't know how this happened," Dr. Valentine moaned with a scowl as he looked around in bewilderment at Hollis's playroom as though he'd been dropped on the planet Mars. Which, considering how funny he looked amidst all the dolls and castles, probably wasn't a reach. "I don't ever remember leaving the hospital. And now I've tried to harm one of my patients? It's unconscionable! This is sheer madness."

"I'll say," Rocky muttered, scratching her head as she watched Dr. Valentine reposition himself in the teeny-tiny chair at a teeny-tiny table she could only assume was Hollis's tea table.

As she stood in Hollis's playroom and Archibald—in a sharp plaid bathrobe—poured Dr. Valentine some tea, Rocky watched the commotion as people wandered in and out, catering to his every need.

Darnell, probably one of the only men in the group who could rival Dr. Valentine in girth, leaned against the far wall, his head pressed to Carl's, who was showing him something with great excitement on his iPad.

Nina and Wanda, their husbands and other assorted family members, gathered in small groups, all talking at once.

She, on the other hand, was skeptical. She couldn't smell magic or whatever Nina had described, but she also still wasn't sure she fully understood the whole magic slant to this, and how Dr. Valentine had been abracadabra'd.

Leaning into Hudson, trying not to sniff his spicy cologne or brush against his muscled arms, she asked, "So let me get this straight. Someone put a spell on Dr. Valentine that made him come here and try to kill Marty?"

Hudson leaned against the doorframe, crossing his arms over his chest. "If I'm hearing right, yep. I think. I don't know."

"I don't get it. According to Wanda and Nina, they can't think of anyone who wants them dead who isn't locked up or dead themselves."

"I don't get it either, but how damn funny is it to see big old crabby pants Dr. Doomsday in a plastic purple chair made for a five-year-old in the middle of this decidedly very pink and purple room?"

Rocky snorted. "Should we selfie and Instagram it? Bet housekeeping would love this turn of events."

Now *Hudson* snorted, but then he sobered, his eyes finding hers. "It's really not his fault. Do you have any idea how damning this could be to his career? If it got out that he tried to kill a patient, even under the influence of magic, the rumor mill would have a bloody field day. He's already on the most-hated list at the hospital."

"Well, it's not like he doesn't deserve to be on that list," she reminded. "He has the bedside manner of Attila the Hun, for gravy's sake."

Hudson's face softened, his expression filled with sympathy. "But he doesn't deserve to go down for something he had no control over, Rocky. He's an excellent surgeon, despite his sour disposition, and let's not forget, he's got some gargoyle disease he refuses to talk about. When you're sick, aren't you a little cranky?"

"Look at you stick up for the meaniebutt," she teased, nudging him in his hard stomach.

"I'm just being truthful. He's got the personality of a rock, but he doesn't deserve to be branded a murderer."

Okay, point for the phoenix, but hold on. As she recovered from her brush with Dr. Valentine, who might not be in good health but was certainly stronger than an ox, Rocky began to try to piece together a motive.

"Why wouldn't this person who put the spell on Dr. Valentine just do it themselves? Why have someone else do it? And one more thing, because spells are involved, does that mean a witch wants to kill Marty?"

"I haven't a clue," Hudson said with a sigh in confusion. "Witches are certainly as good a guess as any, but who knows what other paranormal is capable of putting a spell on another paranormal? I mean, I'm willing to bet there are many species we don't even know about—that we haven't identified yet—who do extraordinary things. But for now, sure, let's say a witch did this. *Why* did a witch do this? And what does that have to do with the list of souls? How does that connect to Marty?"

She decided to ask a few questions of her own. Leaving

Hudson, she approached Dr. Valentine and grabbed one of the small plastic chairs, sitting amongst the dozens of dolls by shelves filled with colorful books, and dropped it down next to him.

His eyes widened in surprise when he realized who she was. "You're the staff member from housekeeping, aren't you?" he asked in soft tones, which, coming from Dr. Valentine, an often loud, blustery fellow, was a surprise.

"Yep. That's me. Rocky McNally—lowly janitor. Listen, Dr. Valentine. I have a few questions, if you don't mind?"

He gave her that condescending glare from beneath his bushy eyebrows he always gave her as he passed in the hallways, before he appeared to remember he was in a pickle. "I don't know what else I can tell you that I haven't told everyone already, but I'll try to oblige."

One thoughtful pause later, Rocky asked, "Well, I figure you owe me one for slamming me against a wall and for this shiner, which I haven't seen yet but I'm pretty sure I won't be able to cover with makeup."

His sigh was gruff and despondent. "Miss McNally, I'm deeply, deeply sorry—"

She held up a hand to stop him. "No apology necessary. Not if what you say is true. Now, I just want to be clear on what I've heard. You don't remember leaving the hospital, putting on a ski mask, climbing up the side of your one-time patient's house, breaking into her bedroom window and pulling her breathing tube from her throat?"

Because magic or not, she was having a really hard time swallowing that bit of information.

Dr. Valentine's hard face went soft as he looked at her, an apology crystal clear in his eyes. "My dear Miss McNally,

I don't remember that at all. I assure you, the last thing I remember was being in my car, preparing to leave for the day. The very next thing I remember is falling to the ground, and Dr. Khalil helping me up off said ground."

Sheesh. He looked really remorseful. He was a hard man, not just in terms of his looks, which were rather blockish and square and granite-esque, but he was hard to like because he was so dismissive.

Seeing him now, with his head hanging low and his eyes so soft and buttery, had her a little unbalanced. She'd never seen him so contrite, and in the month she'd worked at the hospital, she'd certainly never heard him apologize.

Nodding her head, Rocky found she felt sorry for him. "Okay. So do you remember talking to anyone other than your staff or Marty's family and friends about her case? Or have you consulted with any other physicians outside the hospital about it? Has there been anyone unusual hanging around the hospital? Anyone suspicious?"

Suddenly, he sat up straight, revealing a tear in his black turtleneck, his face hard again. His fists, the size of cement blocks, clenched. "I don't know what you're implying here, Miss McNally, but I don't share patient information, not specific information like names or addresses, with anyone but my team. So no. *Absolutely not.* As to anyone suspicious, I deal with all species of the paranormal. Vampires, werewolves, skinwalkers, any number of suspicious characters cross my path during the course of a day."

"Take it easy there, Dr. V. Play nice with the reaper. We like her." Nina slapped him on the back to let him know, in her not-so-subtle way, she was watching.

One bushy eyebrow rose and his eyes widened. "*Is that*

what you are?" he asked, sounding surprised. "A grim reaper?"

She wasn't at all surprised he didn't know what type of paranormal she was. Housekeeping was beneath him. Why would he know their names, let alone their origins?

"Yep. That's what I am. I don't just clean puke and entrails."

Nina cackled and handed her an ice pack for her eye. "We okay here?" she asked, peering down at Dr. Valentine with narrowed eyes.

"We're fine, " Rocky assured her. "I'm just asking a couple of questions."

As Nina took her leave, it was clear Dr. Valentine was done with Rocky and her questions. He rose with a grimace and a grunt, his enormous body unfolding from the small chair as he did. "I don't mean to be rude, Miss McNally, but I have patients to attend to very early in the morning. Are we through here?"

Rocky rose as well, her knees creaking, making her wince in pain. Dr. Valentine dwarfed her by at least three feet, and she wasn't considered short at five-seven. Yet, he made her feel quite small, and she wasn't sure if that was because he was so dismissive or because he was the size of the Jolly Green Giant.

"Just one more thing, Dr. Valentine, and it's kind of personal. I hope you don't mind." She let the question hang in the air until he curtly nodded his consent.

"By all means," he drawled in his arrogant tone.

"I know you're sick. Everyone at the hospital does. What exactly do you have, and why can't it be cured?"

His eyes pinned hers and narrowed. It looked like he was considering whether he deemed her worthy enough to know, and then resigned himself to telling her. "I'm dying of old age, Miss McNally. Gargoyles, unlike you lot, aren't immortal. We simply live for hundreds of years. And as I'm sure you know via the rumors at the hospital, I'm the last of my kind."

Well, wasn't that some shit? He'd managed to make her feel bad about how mean she'd said he was.

Guilt made her reach out and grab his huge hand. He was a jerk, but even jerks needed love. "I'm sorry, Dr. Valentine."

He didn't grab hold of her hand, but he did squeeze ever so lightly before he cleared his throat. "Now, may I be excused?"

Rocky took a step backward and allowed him to pass. "Of course. Have a good night."

With a deep breath inward, she watched him pick his way though the people, shake hands with Archibald and leave the room.

Hudson approached her with a tentative expression. As she looked up at him, trying to hang on to his gaze and not allow his dreamy eyes to suck her into his vortex of sexy, she noticed something was missing around his neck.

Pointing to his neck, she asked, "Hey, where's you're chain?"

Hudson's hand went immediately to his neck. "Damn. It must've fallen off outside when I went after Dr. Valentine. Speaking of, you okay?"

Running a hand through her hair, wincing when she

touched the back of her head where it had slammed against the wall, she blew out a pent-up breath. "No. I feel horrible. That man is sick, and I was ready to grill him like I was one half of Cagney and Lacey. I'm going to bake him some cookies and drop them at the hospital when this is all over to say how sorry I am."

"*You* bake? You?" Hudson sounded surprised.

She made a face at him. "I, unlike you, have hobbies, buddy. I might play Doctor Death on TV, but in my downtime, I need a stress reliever. So yes, I bake. I'm a pretty good cook, I read, I ride my bike. I take spin classes. I even do a little hot yoga."

"So that's what it's like to have a life, huh?" he teased with his gorgeous smile. "Maybe some time you could teach me how to cook. Anything has to be better than those veggie burgers and fruit cocktail cups in the hospital cafeteria."

"First off, veggie burgers? Don't even use the word burger and veggie in the same sentence. Second, why not leave the hospital long enough to take some cooking classes? Maybe make some friends?" she responded evasively.

He nodded his head, his dark hair, no longer slicked back from his face, grazing his sharp chin. "Oh, right. I forgot. You have plenty of friends. My bad."

"That I do—"

"Hey, Reaper?" Nina bellowed from the doorway.

Phew. Saved by the violent vampire. "Yeah?" she yelled back.

"There's someone downstairs who says he's your father.

First, do you have a father? Second, if you don't, you want I should fucking rip his legs off and shove them down his throat?"

Her father? Here? Like, in the same space?

Hello. Unexpected plot twist in the house.

CHAPTER 9

*R*ocky raced down the stairs, her body one big, upright ache, but that didn't stop her. If her father was here, it meant he knew what she was up to. And the only person who could have given her up was Pepper. She was the only person who'd known what her intentions were.

She was going to kill Pepper—if her father didn't kill her first.

As she came to a screeching halt at the bottom of the stairs, she caught a glimpse of herself in the wide entryway mirror, and it wasn't pretty.

Her hair, which had been up in a messy bun on the top of her head, fell sideways, long strands flying about her face. Her eyeball was an interesting shade of dark purple and near black, bulging out at her reflection like a neon sign. She had a split lip, a cut on her cheek, and a smattering of blood across the arm of her sweatshirt.

So seeing as there'd be no hiding her condition, she greeted her father with extra exuberance.

"Daddy! What are you doing here?" she asked cheerfully, racing up to him and throwing her arms around his neck.

Clinton McNally gave her a quick pat on her back before removing her clingy arms from around his neck. Knowing he wasn't one for public displays of affection (or even private displays of affection), she expected nothing less from her distant, super-conservative parent, but it had been worth the attempt at distraction anyway.

Salt-and-pepper hair in a military cut, her tall, lean father looked down at her with disapproval all over his equally lean face. And he looked none too happy.

Not that he ever looked happy—about anything—but most especially not about his darling daughter.

To anyone else, he probably looked pretty calm, but Rocky knew better. On the inside, he was piping hot.

"Roxanne, the car's outside and running. Gather your things and that mutt of yours. It's time for you to go home."

She heard rather than saw everyone gather on the staircase, by the pitter-patter of their feet, and her face went hot and red.

She knew before her attempt to reason with him, her efforts would be futile, but in order to save face, she tried anyway, because it was goddamned humiliating to have your father order you around when you were countless centuries old in front a bunch of people who took no shit from anyone.

Gripping his arm, she gave it a squeeze and smiled at him. "Daddy, why don't you come in for a minute? Maybe have a cup of tea with me while I explain?"

Clinton shook her off his down jacket, bristling at her touch before he set her in front of him, his eyes ablaze with anger. "You heard me, Roxanne. We'll talk about what you're doing and why you're here in the car. Now, don't make me say it again. *Gather your things,*" he said through a clenched jaw.

For all the times he'd been curt with her, for all the hugs she'd missed as a kid, she'd always fought hard not to hold a grudge. She accepted him for who he was. A stern, unaffectionate, almost always angry man, and she'd found a way to work around it for a very long time. She'd skirted the edges of his life as an adult, she kept all her visits to a brief hour, she tried to respect who he was as a person, even though he was an unforgiving, critical man.

But not this time.

This time was far too important to her. Keeping Marty from soul collection was far too important, and she wasn't giving in to his demands. Just this one time, that little voice in her head deserved to be heard.

So she gazed at him, her eyes determined when they locked with his icy ones. *"No."*

Clinton looked at her as though she'd slapped him, his expression so shocked.

Pulling his driving gloves off, he stuffed them into the pocket of his navy down jacket and glared at her for all he was worth. That glare meant she was due for a seething lecture the minute her ass hit the passenger seat of his car.

With one long finger, he pointed to the door as though she hadn't heard him the first time. *"Get in the car, Roxanne McNally."*

"No," she whispered in defiance. "I won't get in the car." She said those words a little louder. "I'm not a teenager, and

I haven't been for many centuries, Dad. I will not get in the car, and I am *not* leaving."

If looks could kill, her handsome, military-esque father would have killed her with the one he gave her. His green eyes flashed all sorts of warnings she promptly ignored. "How dare you speak to me like this, Roxanne!"

Suddenly, Hudson was there, holding out a hand to Clinton. "Sir? I'm Hudson Khalil. *Dr.* Hudson Khalil. Rocky and I work together. It's pretty cold out. Why don't you come into the kitchen and have something warm to drink? Maybe we can all sit down and—"

Clinton refused his hand. Instead, he intensified his glare, only now it was directed at Hudson. "I don't care who you are. I'm here to keep my daughter out of more trouble. Do not interfere in family matters, do you understand me, young man?"

She saw Hudson's nostrils flare and knew she had to prevent him from getting involved. Her dad and an argument were no-win. She didn't want Hudson tangled up in that.

Rocky stepped between them, placing a hand on Hudson's chest. "It's okay. Please. Let me handle this, Hudson," she pleaded before turning to her father. "Daddy? If you don't want to have a rational *conversation*, go home before we both say things we don't mean. I'm not leaving. I'm not a kid you can order around anymore. Now, if you want to talk like adults—which I'll remind you again, is what I am—then let's do it. If not? *Go. Home.*"

"You'll live to regret this, Roxanne," he seethed, yanking his gloves from the pockets of his jacket and stuffing his salt-and-pepper hair under his knit hat with angry hands,

"Will I live to regret doing the right thing? Or will *you* just live to regret having a daughter so willful she embarrasses you? Because that's what this visit feels like. Instead of being proud of me for taking a stand against something wrong—and you know it's wrong—you want me to fall back in line. Well, I have news for you, I won't do it!" she spat back, tears forming in the corner of her eyes. "No, go home."

Clinton inhaled, his lean chest expanding under his coat. "You're breaking all the rules, Roxanne. You know I can't help you if you're being disobedient, and what you're doing here with these people, with this soul you should have long-ago collected—and believe me, I know exactly what you're doing here with this soul and these people—is the biggest rule-breaking ever!" he accused, his voice rising to the level that meant she was in serious reaper trouble.

Squaring her shoulders, Rocky lifted her chin even as it pained her to do so. "What I'm doing is *right*. What's happening to Marty is *wrong*, Daddy. Dead wrong, and I won't let you try to stop me. So you can tattle on me to my superiors, you can out me all you like, but I'm here to tell you, for once in my godforsaken life, I'm going to fight to the death to keep this reap—Marty's reap—from happening. Count on it."

"I don't have to tattle on you, Roxanne," Clinton chided. "Word is already out amongst us, and it won't be long before our superiors get wind of the fact that you haven't handed over a soul. I can't believe it hasn't already! But you know what can happen when they find out. If you take the soul now, maybe we can salvage this."

Her heart clanged against her ribs as she hobbled closer

to him, staring up into his face. "Who told you I was here, Daddy? How did you find me? Was it Pepper?"

"Wait!" Nina shouted, hopping down the stairs in her red flannel footy pajamas. "Let's try and fucking work this out. Seriously, kiddo, how much trouble can you get into if you do this? We should have asked, but I was so damn worried about Marty, I didn't think about how the fuck this could affect you. So, what're we looking at, kiddo?"

Rocky swallowed a gulp of nervous fear, wrapping her arms around her waist, but her father answered the question for her.

Clinton, only a couple of inches taller than Nina, scowled at her. "She could be *shunned*, young lady. Shunned forever! Dropped off on some vacant plane to roam eternity *alone!*"

Nina was about to protest, her surprise at what Rocky was sacrificing clear, but Rocky stopped her.

"Stop! I don't care, Daddy! I hate reaping, and I always have! I don't care if I never take another soul across ever again! But you know what I hate about reaping the most? Taking a soul that should never have been on the list in the first place with no one to make it right—and I won't do it again! Do you hear me? *I won't do it!*"

Nina's dark eyes went soft as she looked to Clinton. "Your kid's a good egg, dude. Come inside and talk to us. Let's work this out."

Clinton's eyes roamed over Nina's face, probably aghast she'd dare speak to him, let alone use crude language. "I don't know *who* you are, but this is a family matter. Plainly speaking, it's none of your business, Miss…?"

"It's just fucking Nina, Pops, and it *is* our business

because your kid's doing something awesome, and if you can't see that with our own damn eyes, then maybe hittin' the bricks is the right fucking thing for you to do." She walked to the door and threw it open, the cold wind pouring inside, bringing with it a pile of dead leaves and some stray flakes of snow.

Clinton gave Rocky one last long glare, his eyes shooting her a million angry messages, before he stomped out the door. "You've been warned, Roxanne. You've been warned!" he bellowed into the wind.

Nina slammed the door shut behind him and instantly turned to her, holding out her arms.

Rocky went into them wordlessly, realizing she'd not only defied her father, but likely run him out of her life forever. And that hurt. It hurt bad. They were all they had.

As she pressed her face to Nina's shoulder, she allowed herself some long-overdue tears. Hot, salty droplets fell to Nina's pajama shirt with watery plops.

And then Wanda was beside her, rubbing her back and giving her a squeeze of reassurance, pushing her tangled hair from her face. "C'mon, honey. Let's go get some warm tea and talk, okay?"

This kind of acceptance was what she'd wanted all her life. How funny that she'd found it with total strangers instead of the person who was supposed to love her the most.

Carl snuck up behind them and thumped her on the shoulder. "Teeaa," he reminded in his slow slur.

As she let them lead her into the kitchen, and Darnell pulled out a chair, wrapping his big arm around her for a quick cuddle against his squishy body, she felt incredible peace and gratitude.

If nothing else, doing what she was doing was out in the open now. Not that it would stop her. In fact, it fueled her desire to set things right, and that allowed her to breathe a little easier.

But she was most grateful for these people, who, just by existing, had given her new life goals. If she had to live for an eternity, she wanted to do it with people like this. That meant it was time for a life overhaul.

When all this was over, she planned to Marie Kondo her entire life and only keep what sparked joy.

~

The next day, Rocky was more than ready to start looking into some of the things she'd been chewing on since her father's uninvited visit. Most importantly, Dr. Valentine.

As gruff and awful as he could be, no one should be alone when they were as sick as he was. She was going to make it her mission to check on him from time to time.

Hudson sat with her at the kitchen table as she scrolled her laptop and everyone else spent some time with Wanda's sister, Casey, who was upstairs chatting with Marty. When she'd tiptoed out of the sitting room to grab some lunch, she'd left them giggling and reminiscing about Casey's accidental turning so long ago.

As she'd made a sandwich and grabbed some Cheerios for Charlie, Rocky had smiled after hearing about how happy Casey was with her mate, Clay, after dealing with demons and a trip to Hell.

There was nothing she enjoyed as much as a good OOPS tale, especially from the mouth of the women of OOPS.

"So what are we looking for exactly?" Hudson asked, taking a sip of his coffee and a bite of the delicious chicken salad Arch had made earlier that morning.

Bouncing Charlie on her knee, Rocky rubbed noses with the baby, who grabbed at her hair with chubby fists. She'd offered to take her from Nina so she could visit with Casey, and she found herself enjoying her time with the tiny vampire/genie.

As the baby gnawed on a teething ring, Rocky nuzzled her cheek and shook her head. "I don't know. Nothing in particular, I guess. I'm just surfing. Sometimes it helps clear my head. I don't know anything about witches or spells, and if Calamity doesn't know anything about a spell like that, and she's a familiar, it's not looking good for a novice like me. I wouldn't even know where to begin."

"Maybe it was a djinn," Hudson suggested. "Jeannie said anything was possible, right?"

Rocky wrinkled her nose. Jeannie *had* said that, but she'd also said it didn't "feel" like a djinn spell.

"Maybe. Either way, we still don't have a motive for wanting Marty on that list. That's not going to help us to identify who put her there. Unless it's just a cosmic mistake. But that's why I'm here. To prevent anyone from collecting her soul until we know for sure."

While Hudson chewed on his sandwich, Rocky fought to keep her eyes on the laptop screen. Their conversation before the mess with Dr. Valentine had rattled her a little.

She didn't want to like him all over again. She already knew she'd liked him enough before, but the time they'd spent together here at Marty's only reinforced her attraction to him.

She liked him enough that his memory had stayed with her for centuries, but she was already breaking enough rules saving Marty. She didn't even want to know what the punishment for dating outside her kind involved. She didn't want to know what could happen to him if anyone found out about it, either.

"So your father," he began, wiping his mouth with a napkin, his eyes thoughtful.

Her heart twisted in a knot at the mention of her dad. "Ah, yes. Taskmaster McNally. What about him?"

"When you go back home, how much trouble are you looking at for not reaping Marty's soul?"

"I already told you, it could be I'll end up shunned or the reaper's version of imprisonment. In other words, left on a deserted plane all alone." She fought an outward cringe over the word in order to put on a brave face, but that was the truth of it.

"Do you think your father's going to give you up to your superiors? Would he really do that? I don't know a lot about family, but all the television and movies I've watched suggests a parent wouldn't do that."

Would her father do that? He was a hardcore badass, but she wasn't one hundred percent sure he'd hand her over. He liked rules and order, but to give her up and tell her superiors where she was? She couldn't say for sure.

She looked down at the surface of the table. "I'd like to say no, but after last night, I don't know. I *do* know someone's alarm bells are going to be set off if I don't hand over a soul sometime soon. It's been over a month now. It won't be long until they come find me, throw me in a two-by-four and send someone else to collect Marty's soul… unless she wakes up or we figure out who put her on the list."

Just then, Archibald trudged into the kitchen with Nina hot on his heels, snow covering his galoshes and his pants.

"Arch, I told you I'd shovel the pathway," Nina groused at him, her pale face annoyed. "You're gonna give yourself a goddamn heart attack lifting all that heavy snow. There are plenty of us here to help you."

He blew out a breath of obvious aggravation. "Mistress Nina, I'm not disabled, fair maiden. Nor am I ever too old to make snow angels with Mistress Hollis. I happened to see the path was covered as we frolicked, thus I did what any good manservant would do and took matters into my own hands. You all tend to Miss Marty, and I'll handle the rest," he blustered.

Nina laughed at his indignation, wrapping an arm around his shoulder and brushing the snow from his wisp of hair. "Oh, pipe down, Manservant. I'm not picking on your damn age. I'm speaking the truth, and I'm just telling you we need you to cook more than we need the pathway cleared. It takes me two seconds to get 'er done." She paused a moment and plucked something from his back.

Nina held it up, the item gleaming under the kitchen lights…and that was when her whole body began to shake, each muscle tight in some invisible grip. "What the hell do you have stuck—"

And then she froze on the spot, her eyes widening before

she clutched the item in the ball of her fist, her knuckles going white.

Rocky rose from her seat as Hudson ran to her, a hint of alarm in his tone. "Nina? What's happening?"

Her fist shook as she appeared to struggle to hold up whatever was in her hand. Her jaw clenched, the muscles in her lean, beautiful face pushing at her skin.

"Miss Nina!" Arch reached up and cupped her chin in alarm. "What's happening?"

Preparing to run and get the others, Rocky gripped Charlie in her arms, but almost as soon as the shaking had begun, it stopped.

When Nina released her fist, she let out a long groan, as though it had hurt to have her muscles so bunched up.

"Mistress Nina? What happened?" Arch asked, running to the table to pull out a chair as Hudson threw her arm around his shoulder and pulled her toward it.

He sat her down with care, kneeling in front of her, his voice calm. "Nina? Tell me what's going on."

She managed to lift her hand, though her movements were jerky and forced, and popped open her fist with a violent shake of her head. "*This*. The fucking second I touched it, I…"

Hudson took the chain from her hand, his eyes wide. "That's my chain. I lost it when I jumped out the window."

Nina rolled her head on her neck, the bones cracking, and then straightened her spine, her eyes looking almost haunted. "That shit's been hit by some nasty magic, dude. I don't know what the fuck that means, but I felt it. Just like I smelled the spell. It deflected some *ugly* magic and whoever hit you with it wants *you* dead."

CHAPTER 10

"*M*e?" Hudson sat back on his haunches in obvious astonishment. "How do you know?"

Nina hopped up from her chair, her pale face hard as she shook her finger. "Listen, I'm part witch. Like I told the reaper, it's a long story, but long story short, I have the ability to cast spells—sort of. I have a shitty wand that I'm even shittier at using, but along the way, since I was turned, I've noticed some stuff that enhances my vampire senses— and feeling shit like this is one of them. That necklace, *your* necklace, was hit with some kind of spell meant for your ass, Birdman. Essentially, it saved you."

Rocky sat Charlie in her high chair, sprinkling more Cheerios on the tray before dropping a kiss on her downy, soft head. "So you're sure someone wants to kill him?"

"I'm goddamn positive. Whoever zapped that necklace is full of some serious venom for your ass, buddy. So who have you pissed off lately?"

Now Hudson reached for the table, bracing himself

against the surface as he took a seat. "I have no idea. I haven't had so much as an argument with anyone in years."

Rocky's heart began to pound in her chest. "Hold on. Where were you when Marty was attacked last night? Were you in your bedroom or in the sitting room with me?"

His head popped up and he cocked it in question. "In the sitting room with you. I fell asleep on the couch and your screams woke me up. Where are we going with this?"

"And *you* were in the bar the night Marty had the stroke and heart attack, right? A stroke and heart attack I've had a gut feeling from the beginning should not have put her on the list of souls for reaping," Rocky said, hearing the accusation in her tone, but unable to stop.

No. Hudson couldn't be a part of this, could he?

No. Why would he want Marty dead?

She dismissed the thought almost as instantly as she'd thought it. He'd done nothing but take care of her from the start.

However, Hudson lifted his square chin, his nostrils flaring. He'd obviously heard the tone in her voice. "What exactly are you saying?"

She ignored his question as her mind raced and she remembered something else. "But Marty was on the list!" Rocky yelled before something else hit her square in the face. "Waitwaitwaitwaitwait! Hold up. I didn't check the list before I left to do the reap. I only looked at the location for pickup. Maybe Marty's name didn't go on the list until the second Hudson was missed and Marty was hit?"

Hudson stood up, towering over her. "But how can that be? You said it yourself, she's an *immortal*, Rocky. Why would her name go on the list at all?"

"Except for that one small technicality. Marty's half-human!" she yelled, making poor Charlie jump. She scooped Charlie up out of the high chair and began bouncing her as she walked, rubbing circles on the baby's back. "The half of her that's human must have triggered something in the cosmos and added her name to the list."

Nina's eyes narrowed as she also began to pace the length of the kitchen's hardwood floor. "So you think the hit was meant for Birdman? Like, someone wants *him* dead, not Marty?" she asked, her voice rising.

The blood in Rocky's veins went icy cold, but the excitement of having a clue kept her mind racing. "It adds up, doesn't it? A spell, one maybe from a witch, if we're to believe that's where the majority of spells come from, and an attempt on what we thought was Marty's life. But maybe it was a failed attempt on *Hudson's* life?" She gasped as all the dots began to connect. "Who would want somebody like you dead?"

He looked them all in the eye, dead on and direct. "As I stand here in front of you, I can't think of anyone who'd want me dead for any reason."

"And I believe you. *But* you've lived a lot of lives, Hudson," Rocky reminded him, grabbing the sippy cup of whatever Charlie drank from the fridge and giving it to her. "Maybe something happened in one of those lives? Maybe you pissed someone off. I mean, how would you know? You can't remember anything about your prior lives. You said so yourself."

Nina looked at them both, bewildered. "Wait, you're fucking reborn over and over, live for five hundred years at a time, but you don't remember *any* of your lives?"

Arch pulled off his jacket. "This feels like the appropriate time for comfort food," he said, setting off deeper into the kitchen, opening and closing cabinets.

Hudson rasped out a breath before he sat back down at the table. "So all of this could be because of me? But her coma..."

Rocky shook her head. "Listen, that may well be a valid state. Maybe this really is all medical—or maybe some of whatever this magic is caught her, too, and she's in a state of...I dunno, stasis or...something. I'm just spitballing ideas."

Sure, it sounded crazy when she said it out loud, but hello, what in this world of the paranormal didn't sound crazy?

"What kind of crazy sci-fi shit is that?" Nina scoffed with a pop of her lips, taking Charlie from Rocky and handing her to Darnell, who'd lumbered into the room.

"What are y'all down here cookin' up?" he asked, his wide, cheerful face full of interest.

Nina dropped a kiss on her little girl's cheek and gave her a quick hug. "I'm gonna go get everybody else. We need as many heads in this game as we can get."

As she took off to gather everyone, Rocky looked to Hudson, who sat totally still in the chair, as confused as he'd been since seeing the necklace.

Guilt ate at her, guilt and sorrow, because if what they thought ended up being true, he was at the center of all this. Knowing what she knew about him, she knew the mere idea would tear him up.

Now it was her turn to ask, "Hudson? Are you okay?"

He moved his head slowly, clearly still shaken. "I don't

know what to say. If this is about me, then I have to find out how to right this, Rocky. I can't be the cause of Marty's condition. If this is my fault..."

Reaching out, she softened and gripped his hand, hating that it felt so good when he entwined her fingers with hers and loving it at the same time. "We don't know that for sure, Hudson. Let's do some research and figure it out. I know we can figure *something* out."

His voice was ragged, pained when he responded, "How can we figure out a woman being in a coma because of me, Rocky? What's to figure out?"

Kneeling in front of him, she brushed his dark hair from his face, loving the lush feel of the strands. "Because OOPS always figures it out. They always do, and if they don't, I will. *Someone* will," she whispered fiercely. "Now, let's get on my laptop, you get on yours, and we're going to start googling you. Maybe you don't think you have a footprint on the Internet, but plenty of places like country records and all sorts of official places do."

"Google me? How is that going to help?"

"Because there's got to be some evidence a Hudson Khalil came into existence at some point, and if there is, I'm going to find it."

~

Six hours, an amazing meal of truffle mac and cheese, fall-off-the-bone baby-back ribs, creamy mashed potatoes, roasted Brussels sprouts, four bottles of wine and some gooey rice pudding with raisins later, Rocky pushed her chair away from the table with an exhausted sigh.

The children had all gone off to listen to Carl read stories and play blocks with them as the adults gathered round the table, each with a laptop, and began to look for any evidence of Hudson's existence other than at the hospital where he now worked.

Greg's head popped up, his deep eyes capturing hers from across the table. "You okay, Rocky? Need a break?"

But she shook her head. She was here for the duration. "No. No, I'm fine. Here's what I don't get, Hudson. How have you avoided social media? I mean, who doesn't have a Facebook page? Who doesn't want to post a picture of what they had for lunch?"

Hudson laughed. "Maybe because I mostly only eat hospital food? Who wants to see a picture of wilted salad and a dry baloney sandwich?"

Archibald filled Hudson's glass with more wine. "We must rectify that, good sir. I shall begin preparing weekly meals for you to stock your freezer. I simply can't bear the idea you eat nothing more nourishing than baloney—dry, no less. It's unseemly."

Hudson tilted his glass in gratitude. "That's not necessary. You have more than enough to take care of with this crew. I choose to eat at the hospital because I'm there a lot, and that's my own fault."

Arch scoffed at him. "I'd be insulted if you didn't accept, Master Hudson. After all you've done for our Marty? I'll not hear absolutely anything but 'here's a copy of the key to my apartment' for an answer."

Hudson smiled warmly at him. "Thanks, Arch. That's more than kind, and more than I deserve."

"Hey." Rocky nudged him, leaning in on her fist. "Does your name change every time you come back or is it always the same?"

"Pretty sure it's always the same. In fact, it was the same after I came back the last time because I ran into someone at a store who recognized me and called me by my name. Said we went to classes together in med school—forty-five years ago."

Sympathy washed over her like a tidal wave. How awful to always be without a past—without any roots. "Was he human or paranormal?"

"Um, demon, if I remember right," Hudson confirmed.

"Okay, so what about the rest of your fucking life, boo? Like your house, cars, your GD toaster, all that shit? You must leave some kind of evidence you existed, right?" Nina asked with a scowl.

Hudson sighed with clear resignation. "Not a shred. When I rise from the ashes, I start all over again. No money, no place to live, nothing, but somehow, I manage to always find a way to do what I love—which is become a doctor."

Nina made a face of disbelief. "Doctoring costs money to get degrees, dude. Where the fuck do you get that kind of cash when you don't even have a place to fucking live?"

Heath raised his hand, his handsome smile cheeky. "Remember when Arch and me turned back into humans and we lost all our vampire money? We lived in a homeless shelter and the only thing we had left was my car, and I let a company for feminine products wrap it for cash? *That's* how. In other words, you become very resourceful."

Hudson pointed at Heath with a grin. "What he said. I'm really resourceful."

Wanda giggled, covering her mouth. "Oh my heavens. Remember that, Nina? Back in the good old days before we formed OOPS?"

Nina chuckled and bobbed her head. "Yeah. That was just before Marty and me turned your ass into the halfsie you fucking are today. Damn, those were some really good times."

This was like a master class in being a member of OOPS, nirvana if Rocky had ever experienced it. "Wait, so all the rumors aren't really rumors? You guys really did turn Wanda, and then she went rabid and Heath had to bite her to stabilize her?"

Greg laughed out loud. "Oh, it's true all right. Do you remember how mad we were at them, Keegan?"

Now Keegan laughed, too, probably for the first time since Rocky had met him, and it warmed her heart. "Damn right, I do, buddy. I wanted to wrap my hands around Marty's gorgeous neck and squeeze, I was so angry. It was some damn risk she took doing that, pack law being what it was. But we got a hell of a golfing trip out of that disaster, eh, Greg? A solid week in Pebble Beach. God, that was some good golfing."

Then they all laughed at the memory, until Nina sobered them with her next words.

"Fuck, I miss the shit out of her. This all started because of her. Everything we have right now is because she just wouldn't fucking give up. She was the first one of us to be turned, and once she figured this shit out, once she understood how to be paranormal, she wouldn't quit. She didn't give up on me or Wanda or anyone who calls that stupid hotline she created from abso-fucking-lutely *nothing*. She always managed to make something out of nothing. All that bullshit sunshine and lollipops she's always spewing, and I never thought I'd say this, but I miss the fuck out of her optimism. I'll do whatever I have to, but I want her back. I *need* her back."

Greg pulled his wife close, resting his chin on the top of her head as she leaned into him. It was Rocky's understanding vampires couldn't cry, but the lack of tears was almost worse for her to witness, and it made her that much more determined to help.

Leaning over the table, she grabbed Nina's hand and squeezed it hard before saying, "Okay, then here's what I've found so far. Hudson's name goes back as far as the sixteen hundreds—at least on the Internet. We might be able to find more information at a library—"

"You mean, like, look in actual books?" Hudson teased with a grin slathered across his handsome face.

Rocky knocked his shoulder with hers, ignoring the butterflies in her belly at their closeness. "Are you one of those people? One of those 'the Internet is evil' people? Listen here, you can have an entire library right at your fingertips any time day or night because of the Internet, which is a good thing in our case. Besides, if we didn't have the Internet, I couldn't show you the hysterical picture of you in a pair of veeery colorful pantaloons."

She held up her laptop and pointed to a picture of a man with the same name who looked just like Hudson would, if he were a really bad painting from the 1600s.

Wanda burst out laughing. "Nice pants, Hudson. You so

fancy," she teased as she lay her head on Heath's shoulder and wiped away the remainder of her tears.

"That is not me," he denied, squinting at the picture with a frown. "I look nothing like that."

Rocky pointed to his name. "It sure is. First of all, he looks just like you. But also, look at what it says right here. Hudson Khalil, personal doctor to the renowned Orvitz family from Europe who, in later years, eventually moved and began a successful business in Buffalo, New York. You know, the people who make those vacuum cleaners? It says you were born in 1656... And died in 1716? You lived until you were sixty..."

"Oh, and then here you are again in 1802, and it says you died in 1854 at fifty-two..." Wanda frowned and sat up in her chair. "Wait, how can this be? If you reincarnate every five hundred years, why are you on record as dying at sixty and fifty-two?"

Rocky's brow furrowed. "That can't be right. How could you have died not only in 1716, but also in 1854? That's only a hundred and thirty-eight years between deaths. And where were you after 1854? The math doesn't add up."

"Oh, oh, oh, shit!" Nina yelped, turning her shiny laptop around to point to an obscure article about the Orvitzs'. "What the actual fuck is *this*? It says you were whacked by a guy named Robert Bertrand in 1854. They hung the dude for killing you."

A cold chill raced along her arms, and Rocky rubbed them to warm them up. "But what happened to you after 1854? Where did you go for a hundred and twenty-five years? You weren't due to reincarnate for another three hundred and seventy-five. If you reincarnate every five hundred years, how is it possible that you died in 1854 and reincarnated again just before I saw you at the In Between in 1979, which would make you forty years old..."

The entire room went silent for a moment—before she realized the huge mistake she'd made by opening her big mouth.

Hudson's fists clenched as he stared at her in astonishment. "But I'm *thirty-nine*, Rocky. I rose from the ashes in a park in 1980. I remember the date distinctly. It was February 28, 1980. But that's not the real question here. The real question is—how do you know me? *How do you know me?*" he repeated through clenched teeth.

Oh, the piper. He always wanted to be paid, didn't he?

And it really was true. No good deed went unpunished.

CHAPTER 11

*S*he could have sworn that night they'd shared was in 1979… Man, her math sucked.

With downcast eyes, Rocky rose from the table, pushed her chair out and said, "Excuse me, please," before she ran out the back door to the patio, sucking in the frigid night air when she stopped just beyond all the toys and patio furniture.

Snow had just begun to fall, tiny flakes coming down at a gentle pace, leaving the midnight-colored sky swollen with heavy clouds.

As she looked out into Keegan and Marty's huge back-yard, watching the limbs of the bare trees become covered in the sparkling powder, she stuck a finger in her mouth to keep from biting her tongue off or screaming.

She really wanted to scream to let out the frustration she'd been feeling for the last month.

How could she have made such an enormous mistake?

As she trudged toward the middle of the lawn, ridicu-lously hoping the farther she walked, the further her problems would get, her sneakers becoming soaked from the effort, she heard Hudson bellow her name.

"Rocky! We need to talk!"

Oh, no, they sure as fuck didn't. They needed to part ways before she caused him more trouble than he deserved. If someone found out she'd talked to him centuries before—and on their last meeting thirty-nine-years ago they'd spent an entire night together at the In Between, what would happen to him? Would they dump him off on some vacant plane for the rest of his days, too? He'd lose everything because of her.

The pound of heavy footsteps said she wasn't going to be able to avoid him. So she turned to face him, and as the snow swirled around them, Hudson stopped in front of her, his eyes searching hers. Eyes filled with confusion and anger and...something else she couldn't pinpoint.

That moment lasted but a second before all the pent-up longing, all the long nights of thinking about no one but him, all the missed hopes and dreams, made her do something she'd never done before in all her adult life.

Grabbing him by the front of his jacket, she stood on tiptoe and kissed him. Placed her lips on his with a sigh of homecoming and kissed him with every ounce of the passion she'd felt since she'd first met him, and since they'd met once more at the In Between forty years ago.

His lips froze at first, caught off guard, but it was only moments before he gathered her in his arms and pried her mouth open with his tongue, sliding the silken surface along hers and kissing her back.

Her hands pushed through his damp hair, her fingers entwined behind his head, pulling him closer, pressing her mouth to his luscious one until she almost couldn't breathe.

And then suddenly they were no longer locked in an embrace when he gasped. Then he was setting her back from him, his hands still on her upper arms, his eyes wide and bewildered.

"What...what just happened? *What the hell did I just see, Rocky?*" He shook his head as though he could shake off something he didn't understand.

Tears formed and fell along her cheeks, revealing centuries of pain and fear, desperation and need. She backed away. She couldn't answer him. How could she tell him she'd been lying to him all along?

But he reached for her, pulling her back to him, gripping her arms, his eyes no longer confused but wild. "Answer me, Rocky. What did I just experience? Why am I seeing you in my head, lying next to me? Why are we kissing and laughing in a place I've never seen before? *Why?*"

Her throat threatened to close up, but his eyes, angry and flashing, forced her to answer. "Because...because we know each other," she murmured.

He blinked in clear disbelief. "*Know each other?*"

"Yes! Yes! Yes! Okay? Yeees!" she sobbed into the howling wind. "We know each other. We've met a couple times over the centuries at the In Between, and as recently as forty-years ago, just before your last rebirth—or what I *thought* was your last rebirth. And...and we had the most amazing night! Sorry, *I* had the most amazing night. Is that what you want to hear, Hudson?"

His jaw went tight and hard as the frigid air blew his dark hair around his face. "I damn well knew it!"

Rocky shook her head and flapped her freezing hands. "Good on you for figuring it out, Sherlock. Now leave me alone. I can get into trouble for telling you that. Is that what you want? Do you want to be right so badly that I'll pay the price for it?" she yelled up at him.

"Explain!" he demanded, jamming his hands into the pockets of his jeans. "Explain what I just saw in my head!"

How could she explain something that meant so much to her? How could she explain something so rich and full? They'd only be words to him. He'd never understand the feeling behind that night.

But she owed him this. This was a man who'd come back to life to nothing—every single time. How could she deny him?

Backing even farther away, she held up a hand and took a deep breath. "I was at the In Between, on my way back from delivering a soul, and you were there. I don't know why, I don't know how, but you reached out to me. You talked to me first. You seemed so lost. How could I ignore you?"

"And?" He fairly seethed the word.

Her chest heaved as she tried to control her breathing. "And then we met again, forty-years ago, and this time, I...I couldn't leave you. I'm not supposed to talk to anyone at the In Between. There's a huge punishment that goes along with interfering, but..."

"But you did!" he hollered as the snow pelted his face. "You did."

She bounced her head in rapid motion. "I did...and it was like we'd always known each other. Even you said so.

So we sat in a field of wildflowers and we talked and...and..."

"*Made love,*" he finished, his tone softening only a little before he straightened. "So all this time, you knew who I was. You knew me at the hospital. You knew I had *no one* and you never said a word. *Not a single damn word.*"

"I swear to you, Hudson, it was for our protection! *Your protection.* I don't know what they'll do to *me,* let alone you if someone found out I messed with a soul at the In Between!"

His eyes narrowed and glittered in the dark night. "And you didn't think you could trust me after everything we shared? You didn't think you could trust I'd never tell anyone? That I'd never hurt you?"

Oh, God. How could she possibly explain that she was more terrified of him knowing what had happened, and of it happening again, here on earth? How could she explain she'd wanted him so much that having him here, so near her in the flesh, was killing her?

So all she could manage was, "I was afraid..."

Hudson didn't say anything. In fact, if looks could kill, she'd likely be six feet under. Bearing his silence was almost harder than not telling him about that night. It meant he was beyond angry.

He took one long, last look at her before he stalked deeper into the backyard, flapped his arms and shifted, the sparks of his shift in brilliant scarlet and gold, lighting up the dark sky and leaving her feeling lonelier than she'd ever felt in all her centuries.

Rocky shuddered a breath in and out, managing to make her way to Hollis's swing set, where she dropped down into a swing and closed her eyes, allowing her tears to flow.

Moments later, she felt a strong hand on her shoulder. "So you knew Hudson in one of his lifetimes?" Nina asked, sitting on the swing next to her and pushing off the frozen ground with her work boots.

Leaning her head against the chain of the swing, Rocky tucked her chin into her sweater and shook her head. "Not in one of his lifetimes. I met him at the In Between. That's where we first met."

Wanda was there, too, her swollen belly jutting forward, her face soft in sympathy. "Oh, right. I remember you telling us about that place. That's the place you walk between life and death. You travel that road to take souls to their final destination, yes?"

"Yes."

As Nina swayed, she gave her a thoughtful look, her coal-black eyes searching Rocky's. "But you're not supposed to talk to anyone when you do it, right?"

Oh, she was so right. If she'd just shut her mouth and never spoken to him that one time, she wouldn't be in this jam right now. "Right. It's...forbidden. I don't know why. Probably because I imagine some people aren't ready to go to their final destinations, and shitty reapers like me are easily swayed with sob stories. Imagine the mess the world would be in if we listened to every serial killer tell us why they shouldn't end up in Hell? But yeah, we *talked*."

"Damn, kid. That's a shitty row to hoe. So what happened? How was he able to talk to you in the first place?"

"I guess because he's a phoenix, he travels that road himself, alone. He doesn't need an escort because he's immortal. But he's a unique immortal, in that he straddles life and death every five hundred years or whatever the time frame is. That he was reincarnated after a hundred and twenty-five years makes no sense to me. But anyway, yes. That's where I first met him."

Nina nodded, her dark hair falling around her face in shiny damp strands. "And he doesn't remember because he forgets all the shit that happens once he's reborn."

She sighed forlornly. "Yeah... But I think he remembers now." Her stomach twisted into a knot as a flash of their kiss settled in her mind's eye.

Wanda tugged on a lock of her hair before tilting Rocky's chin upward, her face filled with sympathy. "That must have been some conversation."

If she only knew... "I shouldn't have done it. I don't even know why I did."

"Because he's gorgeous, Rocky. Who wouldn't stop to talk to him if he talked first? I'd stop even if I were in Hell and Satan were hot on my heels," Wanda said on a chuckle, tucking her sweater around her engorged middle.

"Jesus, Wanda. You're one step away from twirling your hair," Nina said on a laugh.

Wanda flapped her hands at her friend. "Oh, c'mon, vampire. You know it's the truth. If you were single and you had a stab at that piece of beef, you can't tell me you wouldn't take it. He's delicious. All that dark hair and those abs, not to mention, he smells like heaven. I might be an old married woman, but I still have eyeballs, and apparently an abundance of hormones," she said on a tinkling giggle. "Either way, you spoke to him and it's stayed with you, huh?"

"The first time I met him, we only talked for a minute or

two. It's rare to cross paths with another reaper at the In Between, let alone an immortal. But I never forgot him. I mean, who could forget him? But the next time we talked, well…"

"It was all cupcakes with sprinkles and fucking fireworks?" Nina asked as she stopped swinging.

Oh, it had definitely been cupcakes with sprinkles and fucking fireworks. It had been so many other things, too…

Rocky scrunched her eyes shut to fend off tears. "It…it was a lot of things. It was the most in-depth, amazing, intimate conversation I've ever had in my life, and I've had a pretty long life. I've dated a lot of guys, but none like Hudson."

Nina nodded, tucking her long hair into her hoodie and tightening the strings. "I'm gonna go out on a limb and say you two did the smexy? Because that shit changes everything, and you sound like everything changed."

She'd never told a single soul what they'd done. Not one. Not even Pepper, but she found herself nodding as a tear fell from her eye. "We did," she whispered. But then her head shot up. "And even though it was wrong, even though he remembers none of it, not a single moment, I don't regret it. I'll never regret it."

"Well, he sure the fuck looked like he remembered something when you laid that one on him a minute ago, before he stormed off like a big-ass baby."

Rocky couldn't help but chuckle. "You saw?"

Nina gave her a light shove. "Are you fucking kidding? We *all* saw. Who could miss that shit? The only thing missing was Cupid shooting arrows and some bullshit love song playing in the background. And we know Cupid, by the way—in case you need to know for sure if it's really love."

Her eyes went wide as she looked to the vampire. "You know Cupid? The *Cupid*?"

Wanda swatted at Nina. "Oh, hush. Now's not the time. Let's finish talking about where we are now and table all meetings with Cupid until further notice."

"Wanda's right," Nina agreed. "So you've been gaga over this dude for a long time."

"Yes." She breathed out the word, feeling indescribable joy at being able to finally say it out loud.

Wanda ran a gentle hand over her head. "And all this time, all these years, you've been mourning this…this encounter, knowing Hudson wouldn't remember because he was on his way to being reborn and he forgets everything after reincarnation."

"Yes," she managed to say around the tightening of her throat.

"Aw, honey. So why is it you didn't tell him? Why didn't you remind him about what happened?"

"Because it's forbidden. Because reapers are only allowed those kind of relationships with other reapers."

"Says the fuck who?" Nina spat. "You know, they gave me that load of bullshit when I hooked up with Greg. I lost count of how many goddamn times other full-blooded vampires told me I was impure. Fuck that."

"Says my father. You met him. I'm in enough trouble as it is. He'd kill me if I even thought about dating anyone but another reaper. It's cause for termination."

Nina's head shot up, her eyes glittering. "As in kill-you termination, or like job termination?"

"As in shun me to a vacant plane. End of. What my dad told you the other night is true. But it's not me I'm worried so much about. They'd shun my dad, too. I don't always get along with my father, obviously. You saw that for yourselves. But I'm not sure I could put him through that kind of humiliation or isolation. I've never known anyone who's been shunned personally, but I've heard the rumors. At best, they'd only boot him out of the community. It would leave him all alone. So I'd be gone and, worse, he couldn't be with his own kind, either."

Wanda's sigh was wistful. "I wish I could say I'm surprised, but bigotry and discrimination aren't only committed by humans. The paranormal have as many ridiculous rules about life mates as the rest of humanity."

The misery she was feeling right now clawed at her from her toes to the top of her head. "But it's not just about my father, Wanda. I don't know what could happen to Hudson. What if he was sent off to a vacant plane for being involved with me? I couldn't live with myself if he landed on an empty plane for eternity and had to continually reincarnate to nothing and no one. He's already alone as it is, but at least there are other people here."

Nina twisted the swing to face her. "Well, we know for sure how your father feels about this shit after the other night."

Rocky barked a sarcastic laugh. "My father considers a reaper who's been shunned traitors to their own kind. Reaping is a sacred thing. We're the messengers of death, and my father takes that very seriously. He considers it a privilege to walk someone through the In Between, and maybe it is for some. But I *hate* it, and I always have. I've struggled with it. I've questioned it. It's damn clear I wasn't cut out for it, but I also can't put him through the scorn and solitude of a shunning."

"Fucking bullshit is what that is. The shunning shit happens in a vampire clan, too, and it's a reeeal popular way to keep people in line. But most of all, it's a load of bullshit. There's gotta be a way around it."

Rocky shook her head with vehemence. "It doesn't matter anyway. None of it does. I lost track of Hudson when he was reborn. No one was more surprised than I was when I saw him at the hospital. I hadn't seen him in forever, but he didn't remember me anyhow, so it didn't make a difference."

"But now he remembers. He's fucking interested in you *now*, Reaper. He's always making stupid eyes at you when you're not looking. We've all seen it."

Wanda held up her hand to Nina. "So you bear the burden of what you shared with Hudson all alone, and you're afraid to strike up a relationship with him—because trust me when I tell you, Rocky, he'd welcome your attention—due to the rules imposed upon you by your kind?"

In a nutshell, yes. That was exactly the reason. "And by my dad."

"Ain't that some shit. But you'll never get me to believe there's not a way around it. We just have to find it."

Rocky almost smiled—almost—and then she let her eyes fall to the frozen ground. "What difference does it make anyway? He was pretty angry with me, and for the moment, we have bigger fish to fry. So how about we try and figure out why Hudson isn't living out his full five hundred years and who might want him dead?"

"Nice way to deflect," Wanda said, leaning down and giving her a warm, plumeria- scented hug. "We'll table this for now, because you're right. We need to get to the bottom of this. But make no mistake, when we figure out what's going on with Hudson and Marty, we're going to revisit Rocky."

Her stomach sank. There'd likely be nothing to revisit. How would Hudson ever forgive her for not trusting him?

How could she explain that she didn't trust herself?

CHAPTER 12

*T*wo days later, after they'd poked around every corner of the Internet trying to find out who'd killed Hudson in 1716, before Robert Bertrand had killed him and was hanged in 1854, they'd still had no luck.

They also still couldn't explain why he was reincarnating at less than five hundred years, or why Hudson claimed to have been born in 1980 when Rocky distinctly remembered meeting him in 1979.

Nothing added up, and the only thing that remained was that someone had tried to kill him again the night Marty had a stroke and a heart attack.

Worse, he now remembered everything about their time in the In Between because she couldn't keep her lips to herself. So now, every time they passed each other in the hall or sat at a meal, he refused to even look at her, but they both knew what had passed between them.

As she made her way up the stairs toward the bathroom, connecting to Marty's bedroom, which had become her hideout because she still wasn't convinced a reaper wouldn't

145

come for the werewolf, and she figured lying low was her best option with Hudson, she heard Keegan's voice.

Trying to be as respectful as she could, she avoided disturbing what sounded like Keegan doing his daily ritual of sitting with his wife and simply talking to her about his day, but she tripped over Dwight Johnson's stout body, making him yelp.

Cringing, she reached down and put a hand over his muzzle to shush him, using her other hand to pat his belly. "I'm sorry, buddy!"

"Rocky?" he called out, his husky voice floating into the sitting room

"Keegan?"

His dark head shot upward, his eyes red-rimmed and bloodshot, tearing at Rocky's heart. He was so tired. How long could they all keep this up?

"Is everything okay?"

Poking her head into the room, she nodded. "Just me and my clumsy. Sorry to disturb."

"Hey, Rocky. Have you met my wife?" he asked, his handsome face so proud of the beautiful woman who lay so still on the bed, her long blonde hair falling all around her face and shoulders.

Swallowing her emotions, Rocky made herself smile. "You know, in all the time I've been here, I don't think we've been formally introduced."

He motioned her into their beautiful bedroom and patted the chair next to the bed. "Then allow me." He took his wife's hand in his, holding it to his lips. "Marty, honey, this is Rocky McNally. The woman who was supposed to cart you off to someplace I'm sure you would have been curious as all hell to see, but I'm damn glad you didn't."

Rocky smiled at him again, tucking her arms to her chest. "It's a pleasure, Marty, and can I say something here? You guys? You're my idols. I've heard so much about you three. You're a bunch of legends where I come from, and I can't wait until you're well enough to let me gush over all the amazing things you've done."

Keegan's head fell between his shoulders, his chin touching his chest. "She's pretty amazing, isn't she? She's the best accidental decision of my life."

"The amazing-est," Rocky whispered, hoping her voice didn't tremble. "Absolutely the amazing-est."

Shaking off his sadness, he lifted his tired eyes to meet hers. "Hey, listen. I know it's been a rough couple of days for you, with your dad and all. You okay? Do you need anything?"

She reached a hand out and placed it on his broad shoulders. "Everything's fine. I'm fine, but you're *not* fine. So listen, I'm up anyway—all night long. Why don't you take a small break along with everyone else and let me sit with her. If that's okay, I mean. I won't leave her alone. *Promise.*"

Keegan grabbed her hand then and gave it a hard squeeze before letting go. "You're a good soul, Rocky McNally. No matter what happens with..." He paused and swallowed. "No matter what happens with us, with Hudson, you've always got a friend in me and mine. If you ever need anything, all you have to do is say the word and I'm there—*we're* there."

She'd never experienced this kind of loyalty before, not

even from Pepper…or, for that matter, her father. This ride-or-die mentality, and it warmed her heart to overflowing.

Her heart clenched inside her chest. She liked these people so damn much. She liked everything they stood for, and she'd never forget her time with them.

"You know what? Under normal circumstances I'd say thanks in a no-thanks sort of way, but when I say thank you this time, I mean it. No matter what happens, I'd like to stay in touch."

Keegan smiled wearily as he rose and whispered "*always…*" before he took three or four strong strides and left the room, leaving her alone with one of her idols.

Taking Marty's hand for the first time since this had all begun, Rocky squeezed it and closed her eyes, leaning forward to whisper in the werewolf's ear. "You don't know me, Marty, but my name is Rocky, and I'm a reaper. A grim reaper, and I guess I only know you through the stories people tell about you, and through your friends, but I want more than anything for you to live. I was the person who was supposed to take your soul, but I… I just couldn't. You're too important to the world—humans and paranormals alike."

As the life support machines rose and fell, as Marty's chest rose with them, Rocky opened her eyes and gazed at this beautiful woman, so adored by so many, and sent a silent prayer into the universe.

She didn't know if prayer worked, but she was willing to give anything a shot at this point. "I swear to you, I swear on everything I have, which isn't much, mind you, but I'll swear on it anyway, I'm going to do whatever it takes to right this wrong. I just need you to keep fighting, Marty. Wherever you are, keep fighting, and I'll keep fighting, too. Whatever has you in its clutches, fight it with every damn thing you have."

She sat that way for a long time, holding Marty's hand, telling her all about her dilemma with Hudson, about her life, about what she liked to watch on TV and her favorite foods, until Greg came in and offered to relive her.

As she left the opulent bedroom, even though Marty hadn't spoken a word, Rocky somehow felt they'd shared something regardless.

On her way to the bathroom to dry the sudden bout of tears she was having, Rocky heard Hudson's warm, gravelly voice coming from Hollis's gorgeous purple room.

Just the sound of his voice stirred her heart, made her ache from head to toe. She wanted so much to talk to him. To explain why she'd avoided him, but clearly, he needed time to process what he'd remembered.

And how could she blame him? They'd shared something incredible and intimate and she'd been acting as though he were nothing more than an inconvenience. Her only defense was she'd done it to protect him, to protect her father, but that didn't change the pain in her heart or how much she wanted him—or the fact that their kiss had blindsided him.

"Milady." Hudson held up his teacup to Hollis and clinked the purple cup to hers before taking a sip.

Rocky deciphered whatever was in the teacup was probably distasteful to Hudson's taste buds, by the widening of his eyes when he took his first sip, but he swallowed whatever it was like a champ and smiled at the little girl, throwing the fluffy blue feathered boa over his shoulder.

"How delightful!" he cooed in a fake British accent, taking another sip and making a fuss over choosing a sprinkle cookie.

Little Hollis, an exact mini-me of Marty with hair down to her waist, batted her long eyelashes at him and giggled. "Do you really like it?"

Straightening his floppy white hat with the yellow and purple flowers around the brim, he nodded. "It's simply divine," he twittered, followed by a devastatingly handsome smile.

Hollis grinned at him and rose to pour some more then sat back down and cupped her face in her hands, giving him a thoughtful look. "Are you going to fix Mommy?"

Hudson didn't miss a beat, he kept right on smiling, his eyes bright. "I'm sure going to try, Hollis. I promise, I'm going to try as hard as I can."

Hollis looked down at her cup of tea, the fringe of her eyelashes brushing her cheeks. "I miss her a lot. She used to have tea with me all the time."

As a tear began to roll down her cheek, Hudson leaned forward and brushed it away with his gentle fingers. "And that makes you sad, right?"

Hollis nodded her head, her long pigtails bobbing. "Uh-huh. Really, really sad."

Resting his elbows on his knees, Hudson said, "You know, Hollis, it's okay to be sad. If you want to cry, or even if you want to be mad, it's okay. I don't mind a bit."

When Hollis looked up at him, her eyes swollen with unshed tears, Rocky thought for sure she'd die right there—that her heart would explode right from her chest.

"Really? I try not to cry because I don't want my aunties to see or for Mommy to hear or Daddy to be sad, too, but..."

"But sometimes you just have to let it out or you'll explode," he replied, making a blowing-up motion with his fingers, giving her permission, the permission she so clearly needed to let it all go.

And as she began to cry, Hudson rose from his teeny-tiny plastic purple and pink chair, knelt in front of her and wrapped his arms around her small frame. Hollis cried while he swayed back and forth until she was done.

And when Hollis's tears subsided, he wiped her tears with his boa, poured her some more tea and continued their tea party as if he wasn't the most amazing man on the entire planet—and it made Rocky more determined than ever to figure out how to fix this terrible, horrible, very bad thing that had happened to him and Marty.

❧

Hudson made his way back to the kitchen after checking on Marty and his tea with Hollis, planning to make mention that maybe Hollis should see someone professionally about what was happening.

There wasn't a more loved little girl, of that much he was sure. She had a houseful of people who would die for her, but they weren't experts when it came to the inner work-ings of the mind of a little girl whose mother was very sick and unable to communicate.

He thought about that all while he poured himself a cup of coffee and fought to keep from thinking about his personal problem. Not the one about someone wanting him dead. He didn't have a clue who wanted that, and he was so wrapped up in his guilt that Marty had allegedly become mixed up in this because of him, he couldn't attack the issue rationally just yet.

What he was really upset over was Rocky. That pull he felt toward her, that unreasonable, insane desire to kiss her without even knowing who she was, actually wasn't unwarranted at all.

In a sense, he did know her, and if the memories he'd had when she' kissed him—the ones that had rushed through him like a tsunami—were even a small indication of what they'd shared, he felt cheated.

Because even if it had only been one night, their conversation, their lovemaking, had spanned this invisible bridge between them, making it feel as though they'd known one another forever.

And he just couldn't shake that. It had been real. Vivid. And it had filled him up like nothing before.

As angry as he was with her for not telling him who she was, what they'd meant to one another, now that he'd had a couple of days to process what he was feeling, he'd softened.

Rationally, he realized she'd had no idea that kiss would jar his memory. But the kiss had rocked his world, had changed the game entirely, and now that he could see past his haze of anger and disappointment, he realized he wanted more. So much more, and he'd do whatever it took to make that happen.

There had to be a way around this shunning, and he was going to find it—if she'd have him after he'd stormed off like a five-year-old.

"What in all of fucking reincarnation is *this* shit?" Nina

yelped from the living room, where he'd last seen her with her laptop.

He hurried through the kitchen to the living room. "Nina? What's up?"

She held up her laptop. "You're never gonna believe this shit—"

"*Niiinaaa!*" Wanda screamed from the top of the stairs, making them both jump.

"What the hell, Wanda?" Nina yelled back.

Wanda's footsteps sounded on the staircase as she hobbled into the living room as fast as her big belly would allow. "He's got her!" she yelled, running for the door.

Nina's beautiful face went dark and her eyes went wide. "What the fuck are you talking about, Preggers?"

"Someone just drove up in a dark sedan and threw Rocky inside!"

CHAPTER 13

*R*ocky's breathing was strained due to the cloth stuffed in her mouth, and at first she fought it, but then she remembered a show she'd watched where the person had managed to get their tongue around the material and push it out of their mouth.

Instantly, she began to push at the material, fighting her gag reflex while her mind raced

As she managed to open her throbbing eye and get her bearings, Rocky strained against whatever held her in place.

A chair. She was tied to a chair by some scratchy rope, she realized, as whatever she'd been drugged with began to subside, and she felt the hard surface beneath her butt.

Shaking off the residual haze, Rocky really looked around for the first time, her eyes opening wide in horror.

What in all of Michael Myers was this place?

First, it smelled like someone had died and it looked like this was the place they'd done it. Second, there were tons of Bunsen burners and vials and…and…her father…

Her father?

Rocky squinted into the dark space, leaning forward as far as the rope that tied her to the chair allowed to get the lay of the land. The floor was goopy, with dust and debris mixed into the puddles scattered throughout the room. Old gurneys lie in clusters with dusty, torn sheets. IV poles long abandoned sat sprinkled throughout the room, and it was cold. So cold she could see the breath coming from her nostrils…

And that was when she recognized where they were. The old psych ward the hospital intended to tear down and rebuild this year. She'd been on the cleanup crew for the fundraiser they'd held.

Did it get any creepier?

Finally, she managed to push the cloth from her mouth, spitting it out and calling into the dank room, "Daddy? Daddy, is that you?" she squeaked.

There was some rustling before she heard, "Roxanne?"

Using her weight, she tried to lift the chair with her knees and hop it toward the outline of her father. "Daddy! Oh my God, Dad, what did they do to you?"

"*Him.* What *he* did to me." Her father, usually so somber and stoic, neatly dressed and coiffed, coughed, and as her eyes adjusted further, she realized he was bound to a chair, too. "Who is he, Roxanne?" her father rasped.

"Did a man take you, Dad? Are you sure it was a man?" she asked as she managed to get her chair even closer to his.

"Yes. It was a man. The size of a Sherman tank," he hacked out, blood spewing down his shirt. "He grabbed me just outside the house. Steamrolled me, he did. Plowed right into be, covered my mouth with something and knocked me out. When I woke up, I was here, wherever here is. Who is he?"

Rocky could tell he had to push the words out, by the forced movement of his lips.

If she got out of this alive, she was dead meat. He was never going to forgive her for whatever she was mixed up in...and she had a funny feeling it had to do with Marty's reap.

But she still couldn't answer her father's question. "I don't know. I didn't see anything either. One minute I was outside, just catching a breath of fresh air after a tough couple of days, the next, someone was drugging me and stuffing me into a car."

And then she explained her theory on what had happened to Marty and to Hudson, and how this kidnapping was likely connected.

"Oh, Dad, I'm so sorry."

She knew what he was going to say before he said it. *Don't be sorry, Roxanne, be better.*

But he surprised her.

"No, Muffin," he groaned, his tone reflecting his state of misery. "*I'm* sorry. I don't know what's going on here, but I should have realized long ago how much you hate the reap. I wanted to call you after I left the other night. We shouldn't part like that—so angry. Not ever, but..." He cleared his throat. "I'm proud of you, Roxanne. I'm proud of you for standing your ground about this Marty person, and even if I don't always agree with you, I still love you."

Tears pricked her eyes. She'd waited all her life to hear words like that.

"This reap was wrong, Dad. I tried to explain, and I

know you don't understand it all because it's complicated, but I swear to you, it's wrong."

Clinton let his chin fall to his chest, his voice gruff when he said, "I believe you, Muffin. I believe you. I'm sorry I didn't listen."

Another tear slipped from her eye, making it sting. He hadn't called her muffin in hundreds of years. Instantly, her heart clenched and contracted. "Do you mean that, Dad? Seriously?"

"I mean it. If we... *When* we get out of here, we'll talk. I'll talk to whomever I have to and we'll see if we can fix this. Find you something else to do besides collecting souls. I've been so wrong for so long...and I'm sorry."

Rocky made a snap decision then. If she was going to die, she wanted someone to know how she felt not just about hating the reap, but Hudson. The night they'd shared at the In Between was the night she'd fallen in love with him, and she wanted someone to know in case she didn't have the chance to tell him herself.

On a gulp, she whispered, "There's more, Daddy. It's not just about Marty. I...I think I'm in love...and it's not with another reaper."

"The doctor?" he rasped.

She blinked in surprise. "How did you know?"

"Because when a man looks at you the way he did that night, it's obvious. I don't want to know where you met him, but I suspect it was at the In Between." When she began to speak, he stopped her. "No! Don't tell me, Roxanne. I don't want to know the details about the rules you've broken."

Her heart glowed with Clinton's words, but there was

more to consider, like the shunning—her *father's* shunning. "I'll be shunned if anyone finds out, and so will you. But worse, he could face punishment, too. I can't let that happen."

"Not if you met him *after* you left your job as a soul escort and took a desk job…which I'm certain is when your meeting happened," he suggested, his tone sly.

"What?"

His laughter gurgled from deep in his chest. "It's a tough job to fill. No one likes paperwork, Roxanne, and I hear it's piled high at Reaper Central. Why, it's piled so high, I bet you could negotiate your terms of employment with them. I'd also lay bets they're going to be very, very grateful you saved this woman Marty's soul because she's an immortal, and there could be big trouble if her soul's taken by mistake. And I also bet when you negotiate, you could negotiate a nice doctor into your contract. No one has to know when you met him, Muffin."

For the first time in a very long time, she wanted to hug him. Hug him so hard, his eyes bulged from his head. As she wiggled her way even closer, she whispered, "I love you, Daddy."

"And I love you, Muffin."

Once Clinton came into clear view, Rocky had to fight not to gasp. He looked like he'd run into a brick wall. His nose was bleeding, his nostrils covered in dried blood, and he was missing a tooth. His knuckles were scraped and his jacket torn.

"Oh God, Dad," she whispered in fear. As she finally got close enough to him to lock their pinkies together and hold

on for dear life, she asked, "I don't understand why you're mixed up in this!"

"*Insurance*," a voice she recognized said. "I brought your father for insurance. To ensure the doctor who's so sweet on you would show up, and to make sure you'll do what I'm going to ask of *you*, Miss McNally. Or your father dies."

Rocky felt like all the air had been sucked out of her lungs when her eyes met their captor's.

Seriously? Man, had he played her but good. But. Good.

All of them, in fact.

Oooh, if she lived long enough to see Nina again, she was going to give her hell for not smelling deception mixed in with that stupid controlling spell!

"Dr. Valentine?" she squeaked on a gulp.

Out of the shadows, the voice came. Tank-like in size and ominous when he hovered over her, he said, "In the flesh, Miss McNally. In the flesh."

~

"*Are you sure?*" Hudson forced out the words, fighting to keep it together, but visions of Rocky dead somewhere made his stomach turn.

"Am I fucking sure?" Nina yelled in her SUV as they drove to the location Rocky had texted him. "Yes, Birdman, I'm fucking sure! Dr. Valentine is an Ovitz! Don't ask how the fuck I got so lucky, but when I was poking the hell around the family that one obituary said you were a doctor for, I found a picture of you and Dr. Valentine—and his real name is Martin Valentine Ovitz! He was the last living heir to the Ovitz fortune and what we know today as the Ovitz vacuum cleaner company. I'd bet my goddamn immortality *he's* the one who's been killing you before you make the five-hundred-year mark, dude. He wasn't lying when he said he was a dying breed. How he's doing it, I have no clue. How the fuck does a gargoyle get a spell?"

Hudson ran a hand over his jaw, sick with worry he wouldn't be able to get to Rocky in time. And the way they'd left things after she'd kissed him…

Shit. Shit. Shit. Shit!

"If that's the case, then how the hell do I keep rising from the ashes? If he's trying to steal my soul, what's he been doing wrong?"

"You're fucking asking *me*? Dude, I was turned into a vampire because that man in the backseat nicked my hand with his tooth. I don't know how the fuck you keep rising from the ashes, that's not the GD point."

"And now he has Rocky," he muttered dismally, gripping the steering wheel so tight, he had to be careful not to break it.

"Yeah, but you have the five of us," Nina said, thumbing the air toward the backseat, and the men who were more than willing to help him save Rocky.

But fear settled deep in his belly. Rocky's instructions were clear. "She said I should come alone. What if he sees you?"

"That's what every motherfucker who takes a hostage says, Birdman," Nina reminded him. "We've done this before. We'll figure it out when we get there. He's got our kid. The kid who went against her whacked-out reaper kind and refused to take Marty's soul. And she was right, and there's no fucking way I'm gonna let him hurt her. Trust and believe."

Heath reached a hand over the driver's seat and gave Hudson's shoulder a quick thump. "We got you, okay? All of us. Whatever it takes, we won't let him hurt her."

As Hudson came to a screeching halt at the location Rocky had allegedly texted him, he realized it was the abandoned part of the hospital they were preparing to tear down and rebuild. He'd just been to a fundraiser last month to raise money for it.

"This shit looks like the psych ward out of some goddamned horror movie," Nina commented.

As he looked at the gray brick building with the glass doors blown out and a ragged curtain blowing from a window on the second floor under the ominous black sky, he said, "That's because it was."

～

She had to give credit where credit was due. She'd totally believed him when he'd said he had no idea how he'd gotten inside Marty's bedroom. Oh, the shame of her gullibility. She'd never be an honorary member of OOPS at this rate.

Licking her dry lips, she looked up at him and asked, "Man, before you kill me, which I'm pretty sure is on your list of things to do, how the heck did you manage to make yourself smell like you were under a controlling spell?"

He paused for a moment and looked at her thoughtfully. "How did you know I was under the influence of magic?"

"Nina. She can smell magic because she's half witch."

He made a face of disapproval. "That heathen. It's a

wonder her knuckles don't scrape the ground when she walks. And if you must know, it wasn't a controlling spell, Miss McNally. It was a spell designed to strengthen me so I could climb up the side of the house. I'm weak these days, as I'm sure you know."

Yep. She was going to wring Nina's neck. One hundred percent sure, her eye!

"So you were lying the whole time. Ohhh, you're good, Dr. Valentine. So good. You had me hook, line, and gargoyle disease. I really believed you when you said you didn't remember going to Marty's. You looked so remorseful. Was that improv or did you practice those sad eyes? Have you ever considered acting? Because wow and wee—"

Clearly, judging from the size of the veins bulging from his neck, he wasn't open to answering more questions.

"Shut up! Shut your stupid ill-bred mouth!"

"You leave my daughter alone!" Clinton bellowed, but Rocky squeezed his fingers to quiet him.

Rocky shrugged, though her stomach was on full tilt and her heart threatened to push through her rib cage.

"Okay, so you're not into kudos. I get it. Praise makes me uncomfortable, too. But still, I totally believed you when you said you didn't remember what happened to you. Bravo. I'd stand and clap but, you know..." She struggled to lift an arm. "Restraints."

"Why did you interfere?" he groaned, his tank-like body hauling what appeared to be her father's scythe by his side. "Why couldn't you've just gone about your business and let me begin the process of stealing his rebirthing powers?"

Begin the process... "You woke half the house up! How could I help but interfere?" she asked, a strange calm finding its way to her voice—one her belly and her pulse didn't share.

"Bah!" he bellowed his rage. "I knew Hudson would be near Marty's room, but with my health failing the way it is, I've become woefully clumsy, even with magic on my side. I tripped and knocked her tube out, making a damn mess of things, just like every time before. I could never get the spells right, you know. So when that filthy heathen Nina said she smelled magic, I went along with it. And she wasn't wrong, was she? It was magic I had on me. A powerful spell to induce an unconscious state."

Ah. It was all becoming clearer by the second as his wide mouth spewed his words of hatred.

"So that night in the bar, you meant to hit Hudson with this crazy spell and it hit Marty by mistake, didn't it?"

That must have been why Nina saw what she did when she'd held Hudson's necklace. That necklace had somehow deflected the spell and protected him, but hit Marty in the process.

He leaned in close to her, his red nose flaring, his breathing heavy and thick. "Yes!" he thundered. "It was meant to render your doctor friend unconscious! Of course, I would be at the hospital to receive him in his unconscious state, and it would only make sense I'd be his doctor. Me being his mentor and all..."

Rocky's brow furrowed. "But I don't understand. So what if he was unconscious? How could you steal his rebirthing powers?"

Dr. Valentine's whole face went red with rage, his bulky body trembling in anger as he reached into the pocket of his very fancy dress trousers and held up a vial with a crimson liquid inside.

"With this! I'd inject it into his IV line and when he went into cardiac arrest, as he died, as his soul rose from his body, this would allow me to absorb his rebirthing powers as a phoenix and everything would be right again!"

Moving in closer to her father, she placed her hand over his and nudged, hoping he'd know what she was trying to encourage him to do.

Rocky's stomach jolted, and she had to fight not to vomit, but she pressed forward—because her father was managing to cut through her duct-tape with his fingernails.

"But you've tried this before, haven't you? If the history books are right, you tried at least two times before the night at the bar. The problem is, whatever you did, he rose again and you didn't get his powers of rebirth. What makes this time any different?"

Dr. Valentine stomped through the room, his frustration ugly and angry. "You're absolutely right, and every time he came back, I had to find him all over again, try and perfect the spell all over again. *Over and over*, that infernal man rose from the ashes, and I continued to become more and more ill. But this time is different. I *know* it's different!"

As her father's fingers plucked with fury at the sticky tape, Rocky knew she had to keep Dr. Valentine engaged in conversation. "How did you get your hands on spells strong enough to take Hudson's power?"

He shook his block-shaped head. "Spells! Hah! More like dime-store lies I paid hundreds of thousands of dollars for, and when I get my hands on the putrid bastard who sold them to me, when I'm healthy and strong, I'm going to kill him!"

Rocky blanched under the crackling fluorescent light. "The nerve, right? I mean, who does that? Sells you a spell you could get from a Cracker Jack box?"

Dr. Valentine paused for a moment, as though he could enjoy a bit of sympathy, and then he raised the scythe high in the air. "Shut up! All you need to know is I've seen this spell steal another's power. That's all that matters. Now all we have to do is wait for your lover to show up."

Hudson. Her heart throbbed in her chest. "But he doesn't even know where I am."

Now Dr. Valentine dug in his other pocket and pulled out her phone. "Of course he does, Miss McNally. I took the liberty of texting him, and he should be here any minute."

Now her entire body shook. How could she stop this screaming ball of fire from hitting Hudson and imploding?

"So, what's the plan when he get's here?" she asked on a gulp.

He winked and smiled, holding up her father's scythe. "As I said, you're my insurance. If your boy toy doesn't drink this elixir? I'll slice your father's head off. And if he still won't drink it? I'll slice yours off, too."

Yep. That's what you call insurance.

CHAPTER 14

"*S*he's in there. I can smell her," Nina commented, her face angry in the eerie glow of the cloudy night. "That motherfucker. When I get my hands on him, I'm going to chew his legs off."

"Okay, here's the deal," Heath said, and he went about explaining what their plan was.

"Got it. I'll take this end of the building with Darnell and make sure it's clear. Stay in twos in case he has some kind of reinforcements. You guys go wherever Nina's nose takes you and text me the location," Keegan said, heading toward the far end of the gray building with Darnell lumbering behind.

"You okay?" Heath asked Hudson.

His jaw clenched tight. If Nina didn't get to Dr. Valentine first, he'd kill him. With his bare hands, he'd kill the son of a bitch. "I am. Let's do this."

Nina grinned up at Greg from behind her hoodie. "Honey? You ready to kill a bitch?"

"Now, now, my queen," Greg said, dropping a kiss on her

lips. "No entrails for you today. Remember your cholesterol."

She held out her hand to him with a wink and a smile. "God, I love date night. Let's do this, Boo."

As they took off to follow Rocky's scent and possibly create a diversion, he and Heath ran behind them at a slower pace, heading for the front doors of the abandoned facility.

Heath moved like a jaguar, sleek and easy through the dark of night. Thankfully, Hudson was no slowpoke. He didn't have the agility Heath or the others had, but he was pretty quick for a Birdman.

Heath motioned to him to enter slowly, when all he wanted to do was barrel his way inside and find Rocky.

Thank God for leveler heads prevailing, because what happened next could have killed him and horribly injured Heath.

An explosion rocked the interior of the building, followed by several more throughout the facility. Rocks crumbled, and a stream of fire whooshed out in a gush of white-hot rage, knocking them both on their asses.

Whoever this was, he wasn't foolish enough to believe Hudson would come alone, so he'd wired parts of the building as a distraction.

Heath's phone pinged with a text from Keegan. *"Guys! We're stuck here!"*

Heath looked to Hudson, concern in his eyes. "You okay to go in alone? I'll follow as soon as I get them the hell out."

Hudson nodded. "You bet." He knocked Heath on the back before the man set off to find Keegan and Darnell.

And then he heard Dr. Valentine yell from somewhere

above them, " Dr. Khalil, if you want your girlfriend to live, you'd better come in alone!"

If he wasn't so panicked over Rocky, he'd text Nina and tell her she'd been right about Dr. Valentine—with the tongue-out emoji for good measure.

~

When Hudson appeared at the doorway, as everything crumbled around them, Rocky had to fight with every ounce of her being not to scream his name.

"Rocky!" he yelled from across the room, and even from where she sat, she saw his relief.

"Don't move, Dr. Khalil! Stay right where you are because I have a little something for you!" Dr. Valentine said, his voice rich with menace as he held up a shiny instrument.

Clinton continued to pluck at her restrained hands, digging and scraping her flesh until she thought she'd scream, but she managed to keep it together enough to call out, "Do what he says, Hudson!"

She saw the tightening of his jaw, watched as he assessed the room with a mere glance. As he picked his way over the rubble, despite Dr. Valentine's orders not to move, he called back, "Are you all right? Mr. McNally?"

"They're just fine, and they'll continue to be fine as long as you do what you're told, Dr. Khalil."

"It's been you all along, hasn't it, Dr. Valentine? All these years? What do you want from me?" he asked, his voice rock-steady as his gaze met hers and held, sending her all sorts of messages.

But what good would Hudson's calm demeanor do when there was no way anyone else could get in here to help them? The only way into this room was the door. There were no windows, nothing.

So if Hudson had brought reinforcements, they were no good to him, because he might not get Hudson's powers before they could arrive, but he'd surely slice her father's head off, and hers to boot.

Dr. Valentine's eyes narrowed to slits in his head. "You know what I want, Hudson. Of course, you do. But I'll repeat myself for the cheap seats. I want your rebirthing powers. I've tried time and again to steal then from you in order to keep my breed alive, to no avail—until now."

"My powers?" he said, still cool as a cucumber. "How do you plan to get my rebirthing powers when you've failed every other time?"

Oh, sweet Jesus. He was riling the angry gargoyle. For sure they were going to lose their heads now.

"He has an elixir!" Rocky blurted out as her father scraped deeper into her flesh, and she had to bite her lip to keep from screaming. "He has an elixir he's going to make you drink that'll send you go into cardiac arrest and when your soul leaves your body as you die, this elixir will enable him to steal your powers."

"And if I don't drink it?" Hudson asked, his broad chest expanding under his brown leather jacket.

But clearly, Dr. Valentine had had enough talking. He pressed the scythe to her neck, the cool blade humming against her skin. "Take this elixir or I'll slice their damn heads off!" Dr. Valentine screamed at Hudson, saliva forming at the corners of his mouth as he waved the scythe around her head with a haphazard swipe in the air.

And then Hudson was holding out his hand, walking toward Dr. Valentine, stepping over pieces of Sheetrock and fallen IV poles.

"Give it to me," he demanded, his lips a thin line, the muscles in his jaw clenched.

"Hudson, *no!*" she screamed, just as Dr. Valentine grabbed the back of her chair with his block-shaped hand and lifted it up, slamming her down farther away from her father.

"*Shut up!*" he shouted, his eyes suddenly hesitant when he looked to Hudson. "So help me, if you're trying to trick me, Hudson, I'll take her head off, and her father's, too!"

"I said, give it to me," Hudson insisted, his eyes blazing and bright.

And the moment he shoved his hand into Dr. Valentine's space was the moment the building rumbled with an aftershock and the lights went out completely.

Okay, so here was the thing. She didn't have special abilities other than her scythe. She couldn't see at night or smell a pot roast from the next state. She wasn't strong as a football team or as fast as a big cat.

But she was damn well scrappy, and when Dr. Valentine had physically picked her up in the chair and slammed her down, she'd used the force to pop the already-weakened duct-tape off her wrists.

Pulling at the ropes that held her to the chair, she managed to free herself enough that she could slither to the ground and feel for her father's foot.

As Hudson and Dr. Valentine struggled, their grunts mingling with the rumble of the building, she reached her father's foot and crawled her way up.

"Daddy!" she yelled over the rumble of the walls.

"Get out, Roxanne! Get out now!"

Her fingers found the rope around his waist and by feel alone, she began to unravel the knots. "I'm not leaving you!"

"Reaper!" she heard Nina call. Oh, thank God Nina was there! "Stay there! I got you!"

As Rocky was about to turn toward Nina's voice, something knocked her totally sideways, sending her flying across the floor, over crumbling stone and sharp glass, leaving her dazed and stunned.

She heard Nina yell, "Darnell, catch! Throw him the fuck out the window to Greg below!" followed by her father's piercing scream, and then someone was dragging her by the back of her shirt.

"I'll kill her Khalil! I'll tear her damn head off!"

As she struggled, digging her heels into the ground, as tears fell from her eyes and sweat seeped from every pore in her body, she heard voices everywhere, and the clank of something heavy, and then she heard Hudson.

"Stop, Dr. Valentine! Let Rocky go and give me the elixir!"

All motion ceased but the rocking of the building, which was sure to come down around their ears. Dr. Valentine's heavy breathing rasped loudly, and as the lights flickered on, she got a bird's-eye view of the landscape when she craned her neck upward.

He held the elixir out to Hudson with his beefy hand as Nina was just turning around after throwing her father to

Darnell. Heath blasted into the room, heading toward Dr. Valentine with flaring nostrils.

With Dr. Valentine distracted by the commotion, it enabled Rocky to raise her aching arms and slip out of her sweatshirt and his iron grip—and that was when she saw it.

Her father's scythe, fallen to the ground, left in a pile of rubble no more than a couple of feet away.

"*Drink it, Hudson!*" Dr. Valentine seethed the order, handing it over to Hudson, who popped the top off and prepared to tip it upward.

"Noooo!" Rocky screamed, and in one swift motion, snatched the scythe from the floor and swung, the slice through the air making a keening screech of sound just before she knocked the elixir from Hudson's hand and in the process, cut off Dr. Valentine's head, too.

She blinked and put her free hand over her mouth to keep from gagging at the blood as her stomach churned. There was so much blood.

And then she looked up to see Hudson, Nina, Heath and Darnell, rooted to the spot, their jaws unhinged.

Heaving out a trembling breath, she frowned as she looked at the tip of the scythe. "Wow. That's a lot sharper than I thought."

Hudson threw his head back and laughed—laughed so hard, tears fell down his face and he could hardly stand up.

Nina held out a fist for her to bump. "Jesus Christ, kiddo. You got aim."

"Guys?" Heath yelled as the rumbling became even louder. "We need out, now! Grab Rocky, Nina!"

As the building began to crumble around them, Nina didn't appear to think twice. She wrapped her arm around

Rocky's waist, tucked her entire body under her arm and headed for the hallway, where there was a bay of blown-out windows. "Hold on, kiddo!" she ordered.

Her eyes widened in terror as they headed for an open window at full steam. "Wait! You're not going to jump, are *yooouuu?*" she screamed as they whipped downward with everyone else in tow.

When they hit the ground, Nina set her down and brushed off her shirt as Rocky wobbled, gripping Nina's arms. "That's exactly what I'm saying. Now, let's get you in the car. It's freezing and we don't want your little reaper toes to get fucking frostbite."

That was when she saw her poor father, as Greg was making his way to the car.

"Daddy?"

"I'm fine, Roxanne. Everything is okay, honey."

"You threw my father out a window while he was still attached to a chair!" Rocky squealed, as Nina wrapped her arm around her and helped her to the car.

Greg chuckled. "Hey! I caught him. He's fine, aren't you, Mr. McNally?" he asked as he carried her father, still in the chair, under his arm like a sack of potatoes. "No big."

Rocky shook her head at them and laughed a shaky laugh. "That's not what I mean. I mean, where were you two hulks all those years ago when he was grounding me for partying at the coliseum?"

Nina and Greg and even her stern father laughed into the cold night air.

Keegan came up behind them and barked, "Hurry it up, ladies and gents. We don't want to be caught here when this place falls to the ground."

As he said the words, the building began to fall apart in chunks, making Rocky wince and rush alongside Nina to get to the car.

Hudson caught up to them just as they were about to reach Nina's SUV. As Nina tucked her into the backseat, he climbed in next to her and grabbed her hand.

Hudson gave her a serious look. "You saved my life."

"You were willing to save mine, too."

He shrugged comically and wiggled an eyebrow. "All in a day's work."

"I cut someone's head off."

Oh, God. She'd have nightmares for centuries to come.

"Yeah, you did," Nina snickered as she put Rocky's seat belt on her and pinched her cheek.

Hudson leaned into her, pressing his nose to hers as Nina got in the passenger seat and they took off. "Is that like some kind of territorial thing? You know, like cats do when they bring a dead mouse to your doorstep?"

She smiled at him and sighed, trailing a finger over his sharply angled cheek. "Nope. That means we're engaged, right, Daddy?" she teased.

"Right, Muffin!" her father chimed in with a laugh from the last row of seats.

Hudson laughed, too, and then he sobered. "I'm sorry I stormed off the other night. I was just—"

"A man?" she offered, and then she patted his cheek with a chuckle. "It's okay. You were blindsided. I'm sorry I didn't tell you we'd met before."

"So how about we start over?"

She grinned at his handsome face and shoved her hand

between their bodies. "Deal. Hi, Dr. Hudson Khalil. My name is Rocky McNally. Nice to meet you."

"I didn't mean start *over*-over," he teased back.

"Then what did you mean?"

"Well, you did cut off a head for me. We're engaged."

She giggled, her cheeks burning. "And?"

"And this." He angled his head, placing his lips over hers, and kissed her soundly, making her toes curl—right in front of everyone.

Ah, yes.

She understood what *that* meant.

~

*L*ater that night, as they all waited to see if the spell on Marty had begun to wear off since she'd contacted Reaper Central and explained what went down with Dr. Valentine, Rocky kept scanning the list of souls for reaping while fighting to keep her happiness about Hudson quiet.

"So, Marty's name on the list? Did anyone at this Reaper Central mention what went wrong?" Hudson asked as he peered over her shoulder at her phone.

"The only answer I could get out of them was it was an egregious error and someone was in big trouble. The guy I talked to had the gall to compare it to an accident, which he said was kind of ironic, seeing as Marty's turning was an accident, too. And then he laughed and I hung up on him in the loudest way possible when you're on a cell phone and not a landline."

He laughed. "The nerve."

"So do we think the spell caused Marty's stroke and heart attack?" she asked as she kept her eyes on her phone.

Hudson nodded his head, his mouth a thin line. "With the symptoms the ladies said she was experiencing before she ever went to the karaoke bar, like the headaches and such, I'd say the spell wasn't the cause. But I think what put her in the coma and kept her there was the spell. When it rebounded off me, maybe it wasn't as strong as it would have been if it had hit its intended target."

They might not ever have all the answers, but at the very least she'd managed to talk some sense into people.

"And the person who sold the spells and elixir to Dr. Valentine?" she wondered out loud. "Do you think we'll ever know who was responsible?"

Hudson shrugged, his face grim. "I dunno. I do know, I wouldn't want to be the poor bastard if these women find out who's responsible."

Rocky's phone dinged then, and when she looked at the notification, it made her grin. "Marty's name is officially *off* the list!" She almost screamed her joy, holding up her phone to show Hudson with a grin.

He let out a long, ragged sigh and ran a hand through his hair. "Thank God."

Nina came up behind them where they stood outside Marty's bedroom, wrapping her arms around their necks. "Listen, I'm gonna say this shit once and once only. I'm never gonna fuckin' forget what you two did for our girl here. There'll never be enough ways to thank your asses, but thank you just the same. You ever need something, all you gotta do is say my name and I'm there. You especially, Reaper," she said, her voice husky as she dropped a kiss on the top of Rocky's head and gave Hudson a slap on the back before she pushed her way into the room.

Rocky wiped a new crop of tears from her eyes and inhaled, focusing on Marty. "So her breathing tube's out?" she asked, latching onto Hudson's hand to keep him close. She never wanted to be far from him again—or at least not until she got past what had happened with Dr. Valentine.

"Yep. She's only been getting stronger since Dr. Valentine died."

Rocky inhaled, letting it out with a puff of breath as she fought another shiver. "So now what happens?"

He reached down and ruffled Dwight Johnson's head, then kissed the tip of her nose. "Now we wait, honey. Now, we wait."

"Marty?" Nina whispered, husky and raw, reaching for her friend's hand. Then she turned to them, pointing at Marty's fingers. "They moved! I swear to motherfucking Christ, I saw her fingers move!"

Wanda was there in an instant, her fingers running over Marty's forehead. "Wake up, honey. It's time to wake up. We need you. *I* need you. If I ever have this child, he or she will also need you. Please, sweetie."

Hudson pushed his way through the group and grabbed Marty's hand, his face still swollen and bloody from his fight with Dr. Valentine. "Marty? It's Hudson Khalil. You've got a lot of people waiting for you to wake up. Can you hear me? Gimme a squeeze if you can hear me. Open your eyes, Marty," he ordered, his soft voice resonating in Rocky's ears.

Everyone held their breath, their eyes glued to her hand...but she didn't respond.

And then Nina did something—something Rocky would remember for the rest of her days.

"I have an idea. Work with me, folks," she instructed, turning to the home device on Marty's dresser. "Hey, Google, play 'Copacabana' by Barry Manilow. She hates that song. Which is batshit, because hello, Barry Manilow. But if this doesn't wake her ass up, nothing will!"

As the strains of the song began, Nina grabbed a bottle of Marty's bath salts from a mirrored holder in her connecting bathroom and began to shake it like a maraca. "C'mon, Wanda, get in line!" She shook her butt at her friend, who began to laugh as she tried to grab on to the vampire's waist and do the conga.

"C'mon, honey!" Wanda yelled to Heath and the others, as they all sashayed around the room.

"*Copacabaaaaaana—have aaa bananaaa!*" Nina sang off key at the top of her lungs, and even though her throat burned and her eyeball might as well just fall out on the floor for all the good it was doing her, Rocky sang, too.

"His name was Rico, he wore a diamond! But that was thirty years ago, when they used to have a show!"

And then, as though the Heavens opened up and focused all their love and light on Marty, the conga line suddenly stopped, and Greg said, "Wait!"

"*Are you kidding me?*" someone croaked, raspy and dry.

No one moved as they all looked toward the big bed.

"Why are you all in my bedroom staring at me...and *who the hell are you?*" She lifted a shaky hand and pointed it at Rocky. "And worst of all, who had the nads to play 'Copacabana' in, of all places, *my bedroom*? Is their no respect—no decency anymore?" she asked.

And then everyone descended on Marty at once.

Keegan scooped her up and pulled her close, burying his face in her neck, while both Nina and Wanda hugged each other as Wanda sobbed before they all but pushed Keegan out of the way and showered Marty with hugs and kisses she appeared utterly bewildered to receive.

She waved them off with an exasperated sigh before she caught Rocky's gaze. "I still don't know who *you* are. Identify yourself."

Rocky sighed a happy sigh and smiled at Marty, who didn't look at all like someone who'd just spent over a month in a coma after having not one, but two major medical events.

As she approached the bed, she stuck out her hand with a wide grin. "My name is Rocky McNally, and I was sent here to reap your soul. But a funny thing happened on the way to the karaoke bar…"

And while Marty stared up at her with wide blue eyes of shock, everyone else in the room laughed.

And then when they caught their breath, they all laughed some more.

Tonight was for celebrating a la hashtag #Marty-likeits1999.

EPILOGUE

Later that month...

One gorgeous cardiologist/phoenix who'd finally found a place to belong and a woman he belongs with; a grim reaper with a heart bigger than all of the cosmos and the handsomest beau in the universe; the father of that reaper, who was finally learning how to show his daughter how much he truly loved her by taking her to lunch and inviting her and her new boyfriend over to watch *The Walking Dead*; a half vampire, half witch who's never going to stop singing the song 'Don't Fear The Reaper' to her favorite reaper of all; a pretty blonde, no-longer-comatose werewolf who's back on her feet, singing karaoke like a champ and ready to take on the world on her low-sodium, low-carb diet; a very pregnant halfsie, who feels like she's been pregnant for a thousand years and has the swollen ankles to prove it; an assortment of OOPS clients past and present; three adoring husbands, a zombie, a demon, and a passel of children, all gathered together at Marty's amazing home to celebrate a very special first for a very special doctor and to welcome him into the framily...

As he made his way into Marty's crowded living room, filled with the tons of people she'd helped save through OOPS, as well as her family and friends, Hudson grinned. He loved these get-togethers almost as much as he loved Arch's banana pudding. They'd been to two since the mess with Dr. Valentine, and he couldn't wait to do two hundred more.

Since that night when Dr. Valentine had almost taken the one thing he loved in this world, he and Rocky had been together every single moment he was free from the hospital.

He'd made her a priority and cut back on his hours, politely refusing the Chief of Cardiology position. They'd spent their time doing all sorts of things, from riding bikes to watching movies he'd never seen to teaching her how to play golf, and he was finally learning how to use his ultra-high-tech kitchen thanks to her.

And if he didn't already know he loved her after remembering their night at the In Between, he knew it now, as sure as he knew he loved being a doctor, and he wanted Rocky to know he never wanted to be apart from her again.

Slapping Darnell and Arch on the back, he greeted them first. "Gentlemen? How goes the day?"

"Look at you, my doctor friend," Darnell crowed pulling him into a shoulder bump. "Fittin' right in, ain't ya?"

Arch rocked back on his shiny shoes and nodded. "As always, it's wonderful to see you! Tell me, how did you like the new recipe I tried this week?"

He grinned down at Arch. "You mean the meatloaf?

You're kidding, right? How did I like it? It was amazing. In fact, it was so amazing, you've inspired me to try my hand in the kitchen. So it won't be long before you can take a break from all those delicious deliveries you send over every week."

"Bah, it's nothing, Master Hudson. It will always be my pleasure. You and Mistress Rocky saved one of my most beloved family members on the planet. There will never be enough meatloaf for you and your girl."

He leaned into Arch, whispering in his ear, "Speaking of my girl, there's another reason you won't need to send meals my way."

Arch lifted a graying eyebrow in question, "Sir, are you...?"

He patted the pocket of his shirt and grinned, stupidly pleased with himself. "I plan to ask her tonight, and if she says yes, I'm hoping we'll be having dinner together every night for eternity, and maybe with all that time on our hands, she'll teach me how to cook something other than hit dogs."

Arch grabbed his hand and gave it a hard shake. "Oh, sir, what wonderful, wonderful news! Many blessings to you both!"

Rocky pushed her way through a small crowd of OOPS clients, her gaze meeting his as she approached with a warm smile, one he fell in love with over and over. She held up two glasses. "Hey, handsome. I bring the nectar of the gods, otherwise known as red wine."

Hudson wrapped an arm around her waist and hauled her close, letting his eyes soak in her shiny chestnut hair, falling around her face from her messy bun, and her cute floral dress that accented her waist and swished around her legs.

He would never tire of pulling her body to his. Dropping a kiss on her soft lips, he whispered, "I saw you talking to Esther. *The mermaid*," he gushed. "Did you ask her what it's like to have a tail and talk underwater? I can't think of anything cooler."

Rocky rolled her eyes at him and pinched his cheek. "I did not. She's not one of your sci-fi shows, buddy. Now, the ladies and I have a little surprise for you. You up for it?"

He leaned back in her embrace and smiled. "A surprise? What are you up to now? Is it another tiara and sash that says Best Doctor Ever on it? Because while I love the sentiment, I think a tiara isn't in my color wheel."

Rocky tipped her head back, revealing her creamy throat, and laughed, a sound he loved hearing every day of his life.

"It's not anything as pretty as a tiara. But it is something you'll *always* remember."

"I think we both know, remembering isn't my strong suit. I mean, I didn't remember you until you wailed me with that big, sloppy smooch," he teased.

He worried a lot about that. Sure, living for five hundred years was a long time, but they both were immortal. Did she really want to have to remind him over and over who she was, and what she meant to him, after he reincarnated—like, forever?

He hoped she'd give him at least the next five hundred years to prove he was worth waiting for.

She raised a fist at him. "I'll give you sloppy, buddy, right in your kisser."

He laughed, pulling her fist to his mouth to nibble her fingers.

"Now, I have a question for you. Do you trust me?" she asked with a secretive smile?

"Always," he whispered back against her hair.

Clapping her hands in glee, she waved Nina, Wanda, and a glowing Marty over to their corner in the living room, then she turned to him and grabbed his hands.

"It doesn't matter if you don't remember us or anything, for that matter, Hudson. *I'll* remember. We'll all remember for you, and when you reincarnate five hundred years from now, I'll be waiting. I'll remind you who you are. Who *we* are. Look…" She pointed to her phone. "Scroll the photos and the video."

As he touched the app on her phone, a video played, of all of them sitting around the table, laughing and joking when Arch had creamed them all at a rousing game of Jenga by Matrixing his Jenga piece out of the pile.

And another with him and Hollis, Nina, Darnell and Carl, making snow angels and laughing themselves silly, while Wanda called to them from the door of Marty's to come in and have some hot chocolate.

Hudson smiled at the memories he was making, his throat tightening. Despite everything that had happened, he'd never felt more included in his life than he had with these people.

Then there were pictures of everyone, a bunch of them Rocky had taken during Marty's recuperation as she'd grown stronger, during her physical therapy, and several from the time they'd marked Marty's one-month mile-stone of health by throwing her a party, where she'd donned his lab coat and stethoscope as a joke while they ate cake.

Hudson shook his head, incapable of speaking. These people... These people had invited him into their world, and he'd never be able to express his gratitude.

He belonged somewhere with them—with Rocky, who really loved her new desk job at Reaper Central that she'd managed to negotiate after saving the cosmos from one of the biggest mistakes ever made in reaping history.

How could he ever thank them for giving him the one thing he'd been missing for centuries? *A framily.*

Running a hand through his hair, he looked at them—all of them—in astonishment. "I... You mean like that movie we watched, *50 First Dates.*"

Rocky grinned, her raspberry lips sliding upward. "Just like that, except you're way cuter than Adam Sandler."

He began to speak, but he found it almost impossible to manage more than, "I don't know what to...how to thank..."

Wanda reached up and pressed a finger to the corner of his mouth. "You don't have to. Just know we'll be there with bells on. I mean, as long as no one has a stroke, or a heart attack, or ends up in a coma in the next five hundred years."

Marty's laughter tinkled in his ears as she threw her arms around his neck and squeezed him tight. "There will never be enough ways to say thank you to *you*, Dr. Sexypants, but I've got five hundred years to find as many as possible."

"Actually, it's like four hundred and sixty-nine. I've been back in this reincarnation for thirty-nine years."

Nina knocked his shoulder with the heel of her hand.

"Are you fucking telling me you don't know when your goddamn birthday is?"

As he realized what she said was true, he nodded, pulling Rocky close to him. "I guess I never felt like it was a birthday-birthday. You know, with cake and candles? It's just the day I rise from the ashes. I only happen to remember the date of my last reincarnation because I rose by a newspaper stand."

"Well, Birdman? Today's your lucky fucking day, because guess what? From here on out, on this day every year, we're going to celebrate the shit out of you," Nina said with a grin and a slap on his back.

At that moment, Carl burst from Marty's kitchen, an enormous sheet cake with a blazing batch of candles on a cart pushed by his duct-taped hands. "Haaappy… Haaappy birthdaaay," he began to sing, and everyone else joined in.

And there was laughter and clapping, and babies and happy couples, and lots of cake and, above all, when the singing and eating was done, there was Rocky.

He didn't know it was possible to care about so many people.

"Hey." She stood on tiptoe and tweaked the elastic chin-strap on his birthday hat and whispered in his ear, "Have I told you that I love you yet today?"

He pulled the ring from his pocket and held it up, the gleam catching the firelight in the huge fireplace. "Have I told you that I love you back?"

Rocky cocked her head, her eyes filling with tears as she cupped his jaw, running her thumb over it, *"Really?"*

Hudson pulled her into his arms. "Yep. Really. So will

you have me? Five hundred years is a mighty long time to be attached to one guy."

Rocky held out her finger so he could slip it on, and then threw her arms around his neck, kissing his lips, her eyes bright with happiness. "It sure is, Birdman, a mighty long time indeed, but you know what that means, don't you?"

"What does that mean, Miss McNally?"

She gave him an impish grin. "It means I have at least two hundred years to plan the biggest wedding the cosmos has ever seen. How do you think Nina will feel about wearing yellow for a bridesmaid's dress?"

"No fucking way, Reaper!" he heard his favorite vampire yell from across the room.

Nina's yelling and swearing was music to Hudson's ears.

And that was how he knew he was exactly where he was meant to be.

The End

(I so hope you enjoyed this little foray back into the lives of the women who started this all and I really hope you'll join me when we venture back into our normal format with The Accidental Unicorn—coming soon!)

Chapter 1

"Left, Stevie! Left!" my familiar, Belfry, bellowed, flapping his teeny bat wings in a rhythmic whir against the lash of wind and rain. "No, your other left! If you don't get this right sometime soon, we're gonna end up resurrecting the entire population of hell!"

I repositioned him in the air, moving my hand to the left, my fingers and arms aching as the icy rains of Seattle in February battered my face and my last clean outfit. "Are you sure it was *here* that the voice led you? Like right in this spot? Why would a ghost choose a cliff on a hill in the middle of Ebenezer Falls as a place to strike up a conversation?"

"Stevie Cartwright, in your former witch life, did the ghosts you once spent more time with than the living always choose convenient locales to do their talking? As I recall, that loose screw Ferdinand Santos decided to make an appearance at the gynecologist. Remember? It was all stirrups and forceps and gabbing about you going to his wife to tell her where he hid the toenail clippers. That's only one example. Shall I list more?"

Sometimes, in my former life as a witch, those who'd gone to the Great Beyond contacted me to help them settle up a score, or reveal information they took to the grave but felt guilty about taking. Some scores and guilty consciences were worthier than others.

"Fine. Let's forget about convenience and settle for getting the job done because it's forty degrees and dropping, you're going to catch your death, and I can't spend all day on a rainy cliff just because you're sure someone is trying to contact me using *you* as my conduit. You aren't like rabbit ears on a TV, buddy. And let's not forget the fact that we're unemployed, if you'll recall. We need a job, Belfry. We need big, big job before my savings turns to ashes and joins the pile that was once known as my life."

"Higher!" he demanded. Then he asked, "Speaking of ashes, on a scale of one to ten, how much do you hate Baba Yaga today? You know, now that we're a month into this witchless gig?"

Losing my witch powers was a sore subject I tried in quiet desperation to keep on the inside.

I puffed an icy breath from my lips, creating a spray from the rain splashing into my mouth. "I don't hate Baba," I replied easily.

Almost too easily.

The answer had become second nature. I responded the same way every time anyone asked when referring to the witch community's fearless, ageless leader, Baba Yaga, who'd shunned me right out of my former life in Paris, Texas, and back to my roots in a suburb of Seattle.

I won't lie. That had been the single most painful moment of my life. I didn't think anything could top being left at the altar by Warren the Wayward Warlock. Forget losing a fiancé. I had the witch literally slapped right out of me. I lost my entire being. Everything I've ever known.

Belfry made his wings flap harder and tipped his head to the right, pushing his tiny skull into the wind. "But you no likey. Baba booted you out of Paris, Stevie. Shunned you like you'd never even existed."

Paris was the place to be for a witch if living out loud was your thing. There was no hiding your magic, no fear of a human uprising or being burned at the stake out of paranoia. Everyone in the small town of Paris was paranormal, though primarily it was made up of my own kind.

Some witches are just as happy living where humans are the majority of the population. They don't mind keeping their powers a secret, but I came to love carrying around my wand in my back pocket just as naturally as I'd carry my lipstick in my purse.

I really loved the freedom to practice white magic anywhere I wanted within the confines of Paris and its rules, even if I didn't love feeling like I lived two feet from the fiery jaws of Satan.

But Belfry had taken my ousting from the witch community much harder than me—or maybe I should say he's more vocal about it than me.

So I had to ask. "Do you keep bringing up my universal shunning to poke at me, because you get a kick out of seeing my eyes at their puffiest after a good, hard cry? Or do you ask to test the waters because there's some witch event Baba's hosting that you want to go to with all your little familiar friends and you know the subject is a sore one for me this early in the 'Stevie isn't a witch anymore' game?"

Belfry's small body trembled. "You hurt my soul, Cruel One. I would never tease about something so delicate. It's neither. As your familiar, it's my job to know where your emotions rank. I can't read you like I used to because—"

"Because I'm not on the same wavelength as you. Our connection is weak and my witchy aura is fading. Yadda, yadda, yadda. I get it. Listen, Bel, I don't hate BY. She's a good leader. On the other hand, I'm not inviting her over for girls' night and braiding her hair either. She did what she had to in accordance with the white witch way. I also get that. She's the head witch in charge and it's her duty to protect the community."

"Protect-schmotect. She was over you like a champion hurdler. In a half second flat."

Belfry was bitter-schmitter.

"Things have been dicey in Paris as of late, with a lot of change going on. You know that as well as I do. I just happened to be unlucky enough to be the proverbial straw to break Baba's camel back. She made me the example to show everyone how she protects us...er, *them*. So could we not talk about her or my defunct powers or my old life anymore? Because if we don't look to the future and get me employed, we're going to have to make curtains out of your tiny wings to cover the window of our box under the bridge."

"Wait! There he is! Hold steady, Stevie!" he yelled into the wind.

We were out on this cliff in the town I'd grown up in because Belfry claimed someone from the afterlife—someone British—was trying to contact me, and as he followed the voice, it was clearest here. In the freezing rain...

Also in my former life, from time to time, I'd helped those who'd passed on solve a mystery. Now that I was unavailable for comment, they tried reaching me via Belfry.

The connection was always hazy and muddled, it came and went, broken and spotty, but Belfry wasn't ready to let go of our former life. So more often than not, over the last month since I'd been booted from the community, as the afterlife grew anxious about my vacancy, the dearly departed sought any means to connect with me.

Belfry was the most recent "any means."

"Madam *Who?*" Belfry squeaked in his munchkin voice, startling me. "Listen up, matey, when you contact a medium, you gotta turn up the volume!"

"Belfryyy!" I yelled when a strong wind picked up, lashing at my face and making my eyes tear. "This is moving toward ridiculous. Just tell whoever it is that I can't come to the phone right now due to poverty!"

He shrugged me off with an impatient flap of his wings. "Wait! Just one more sec—what's that? *Zoltar?* What in all the bloomin' afterlife is a Zoltar?" Belfry paused and, I'd bet, held his breath while he waited for an answer—and then he let out a long, exasperated squeal of frustration before his tiny body went limp.

Which panicked me. Belfry was prone to drama-ish tendencies at the best of times, but the effort he was putting into being my conduit of sorts had been taking a toll. He was all I had, my last connection to anything supernatural. I couldn't bear losing him.

So I yanked him to my chest and tucked him into my soaking-wet sweater as I made a break for the hotel we were a week from being evicted right out of.

"Belfry!" I clung to his tiny body, rubbing my thumbs over the backs of his wings.

Belfry is a cotton ball bat. He's two inches from wing to wing of pure white bigmouth and minute yellow ears and snout, with origins stemming from Honduras, Nicaragua, and Costa Rica, where it's warm and humid.

Since we'd moved here to Seattle from the blazing-hot sun of Paris, Texas, he'd struggled with the cooler weather.

I was always finding ways to keep him warm, and now that he'd taxed himself by staying too long in the crappy weather we were having, plus using all his familiar energy to figure out who was trying to contact me, his wee self had gone into overload.

I reached for the credit card key to our hotel room in my skirt pocket and swiped it, my hands shaking. Slamming the door shut with the heel of my foot, I ran to the bathroom, flipped on the lights and set Belfry on a fresh white towel. His tiny body curled inward, leaving his wings tucked under him as pinhead-sized drops of water dripped on the towel.

Grabbing the blow dryer on the wall, I turned the setting to low and began swishing it over him from a safe distance so as not to knock him off the vanity top. "Belfry! Don't you poop on me now, buddy. I need you!" Using my index and my thumb, I rubbed along his rounded back, willing warmth into him.

"To the right," he ordered.

My fingers stiffened as my eyes narrowed, but I kept rubbing just in case.

He groaned. "Ahh, yeah. Riiight there."

"Belfry?"

"Yes, Wicked One?"

"Not the time to test my devotion."

"Are you fragile?"

"I wouldn't use the word fragile. But I would use mildly agitated and maybe even raw. If you're just joking around, knock it off. I've had all I can take in the way of shocks and upset this month."

He used his wings to push upward to stare at me with his melty chocolate eyes. "I wasn't testing your devotion. I was just depleted. Whoever this guy is, trying to get you on the line, he's determined. How did you manage to keep your fresh, dewy appearance with all that squawking in your ears all the time?"

I shrugged my shoulders and avoided my reflection in the mirror over the vanity. I didn't look so fresh and dewy anymore, and I knew it. I looked tired and devoid of interest in most everything around me. The bags under my eyes announced it to the world.

"We need to find a job, Belfry. We have exactly a week before my savings account is on E."

"So no lavish spending. Does that mean I'm stuck with the very average Granny Smith for dinner versus, say, a yummy pomegranate?"

I chuckled because I couldn't help it. I knew my laughter egged him on, but he was the reason I still got up every morning. Not that I'd ever tell him as much.

I reached for another towel and dried my hair, hoping it

wouldn't frizz. "You get whatever is on the discount rack, buddy. Which should be incentive enough for you to help me find a job, lest you forgot how ripe those discounted bananas from the whole foods store really were."

"Bleh. Okay. Job. Onward ho. Got any leads?"

"The pharmacy in the center of town is looking for a cashier. It won't get us a cute house at the end of a cul-de-sac, but it'll pay for a decent enough studio. Do you want to come with or stay here and rest your weary wings?"

"Where you go, I go. I'm the tuna to your mayo."

"You have to stay in my purse, Belfry," I warned, scooping him up with two fingers to bring him to the closet with me to help me choose an outfit. "You can't wander out like you did at the farmers' market. I thought that jelly vendor was going to faint. This isn't Paris anymore. No one knows I'm a witch—" I sighed. "*Was* a witch, and no one especially knows you're a talking bat. Seattle is eclectic and all about the freedom to be you, but they haven't graduated to letting ex-witches leash their chatty bats outside of restaurants just yet."

"I got carried away. I heard 'mango chutney' and lost my teensy mind. I promise to stay in the dark hovel you call a purse—even if the British guy contacts me again."

"Forget the British guy and help me decide. Red Anne Klein skirt and matching jacket, or the less formal Blue Fly jeans and Gucci silk shirt in teal."

"You're not interviewing with Karl Lagerfeld. You're interviewing to sling sundries. Gum, potato chips, *People* magazine, maybe the occasional script for Viagra."

"It's an organic pharmacy right in that kitschy little knoll in town where all the food trucks and tattoo shops are. I'm not sure they make all-natural Viagra, but you sure sound disappointed we might have a roof over our heads."

"I'm disappointed you probably won't be wearing all those cute vintage clothes you're always buying at the thrift store if you work in a pharmacy."

"I haven't gotten the job yet, and if I do, I guess I'll just be the cutest cashier ever."

I decided on the Ann Klein. It never hurt to bring a touch of understated class, especially when the class had only cost me a total of twelve dollars.

As I laid out my wet clothes to dry on the tub and went about the business of putting on my best interview facade, I tried not to think about Belfry's broken communication with the British guy. There were times as a witch when I'd toiled over the souls who needed closure, sometimes to my detriment.

But I couldn't waste energy fretting over what I couldn't fix. And if British Guy was hoping I could help him now, he was sorely misinformed.

Maybe the next time Belfry had an otherworldly connection, I'd ask him to put everyone in the afterlife on notice that Stevie Louise Cartwright was out of order.

Grabbing my purse from the hook on the back of the bathroom door, I smoothed my hands over my skirt and squared my shoulders.

"You ready, Belfry?"

"As I'll ever be."

"Ready, set, job!"

As I grabbed my raincoat and tucked Belfry into my purse, I sent up a silent prayer to the universe that my unemployed days were numbered.

NOTE FROM DAKOTA

I do hope you enjoyed this book, I'd so appreciate it if you'd help others enjoy it, too.

Recommend it. Please help other readers find this book by recommending it.

Review it. Please tell other readers why you liked this book by reviewing it at online retailers or your blog. Reader reviews help my books continue to be valued by distributors/resellers. I adore each and every reader who takes the time to write one!

If you love the book or leave a review, please email **dakota@dakotacassidy.com** so I can thank you with a personal email. Your support means more than you'll ever know! Thank you!

ABOUT THE AUTHOR

Dakota Cassidy is a USA Today bestselling author with over thirty books. She writes laugh-out-loud cozy mysteries, romantic comedy, grab-some-ice erotic romance, hot and sexy alpha males, paranormal shifters, contemporary kick-ass women, and more.

Dakota was invited by Bravo TV to be the Bravoholic for a week, wherein she snarked the hell out of all the Bravo shows. She received a starred review from Publishers Weekly for Talk Dirty to Me, won a Romantic Times Reviewers' Choice Award for Kiss and Hell, along with many review site recommended reads and reviewer top pick awards.

Dakota lives in the gorgeous state of Oregon with her real-life hero and her dogs, and she loves hearing from readers!

OTHER BOOKS BY DAKOTA CASSIDY

Visit Dakota's website at http://www.dakotacassidy.com for more information.

A Lemon Layne Mystery, a Contemporary Cozy Mystery Series

1. Prawn of the Dead

2. Play That Funky Music White Koi

3. Total Eclipse of the Carp

Witchless In Seattle Mysteries, a Paranormal Cozy Mystery series

1. Witch Slapped

2. Quit Your Witchin'

3. Dewitched

4. The Old Witcheroo

5. How the Witch Stole Christmas

6. Ain't Love a Witch

7. Good Witch Hunting

8. Witch Way Did He Go?

Nun of Your Business Mysteries, a Paranormal Cozy Mystery series

1. Then There Were Nun

2. Hit and Nun

3. House of The Rising Nun

Wolf Mates, a Paranormal Romantic Comedy series

1. An American Werewolf In Hoboken

2. What's New, Pussycat?

3. Gotta Have Faith

4. Moves Like Jagger

5. Bad Case of Loving You

A Paris, Texas Romance, a Paranormal Romantic Comedy series

1. Witched At Birth

2. What Not to Were

3. Witch Is the New Black

4. White Witchmas

Non-Series

Whose Bride Is She Anyway?

Polanski Brothers: Home of Eternal Rest

Sexy Lips 66

Accidentally Paranormal, a Paranormal Romantic Comedy series

Interview With an Accidental—a free introductory guide to the girls of the Accidentals!

1. The Accidental Werewolf

2. Accidentally Dead

3. The Accidental Human

4. Accidentally Demonic

5. Accidentally Catty

6. Accidentally Dead, Again

7. The Accidental Genie

8. The Accidental Werewolf 2: Something About Harry

9. The Accidental Dragon

10. Accidentally Aphrodite

11. Accidentally Ever After

12. Bearly Accidental

Made in the USA
San Bernardino, CA
01 June 2019